With All My Love, I Wait

Gloria Panzera

With All My Love, I Wait

Gloria Panzera

Contents

To...

Mother, who I miss every. single. day.

Justin, my favorite human.

August, you bring the light and the joy and best squeezes.

Prologue

The letter had been sent.

Raffaele wrote the letter not knowing that the preparations for Liliana's wedding had been made. It traveled from Venezuela crossing the Atlantic, then the Mediterranean. It looked just like any other letter; there was nothing extraordinary about the sheer papered envelope that boasted a blue, red, and white striped border. It may have traveled with haste had the post office been aware of its urgency. Had Raffaele known that Liliana would not be retrieving the letter from the mailbox herself, he may have sent it sooner. And so, this letter in a first-class envelope that had to travel far traveled slowly, stopping first in Miami resting in a hot, un-air-conditioned post office for months. An office with condensation on the walls, and palmetto bugs that crawled in and out of the office unnoticed. The Miami post office waited for more letters needing to travel to Europe before processing his. Raffaele's letter sat and sat, nestled alongside other letters for months in a rather large box labeled "overseas." When the post office manager in Miami decided there were enough letters to warrant a trip abroad, the letter was sent. It then landed in France where it was processed quickly. Later, it arrived in Rome where the Italian post office workers, notorious for their laziness, ignored its existence. It took an overly ambitious worker, who was later fired, to process the letter where it was sent to Campobasso, the capital of the Molise region in Italy. Then on the day of Liliana's wedding, the letter arrived at her parents' house as she prepared to marry Domenico.

The postman rode by bicycle up the roads that wound around the mountain's sides. The road ending in Gildone required the postman to pedal hard and fast as the wind this time of year pushed against him trying to prevent his arrival. He would later appreciate this wind on his way down the road. The postman parked his bicycle in the center of town and began delivering the mail on foot. The town was quiet as they prepared to go to the church to watch Liliana finally wed. The postman started on via San Giovanni and ended on Liliana's street via Farinacci, named for her great-great-great-grandfather who had at one time owned the only bakery in Gildone. There was now a second bakery two blocks from the Farinacci bakery that competed with her family's. The new bakery had created a great divide in the town, giving the people, especially the women, something more to prattle about. As the postman stopped in front of the Farinacci home he smiled, seeing the flowers that were delicately placed around the door. He knocked, and as he did so, Liliana's mother, Amara, answered. She was not known for her amiable attitude, and as she opened the door, she smiled as if she had a lemon in her mouth, grabbed the letter, and closed the door.

She took the letter and hid it in the apron that protected her from the *antipasto* she was preparing. The guests would be arriving soon, maybe too soon, to congratulate her on Liliana's wedding, then, as a group, they would march towards the church. She stood in the kitchen staring at the prosciutto e *melone*, bruschetta, pizza laced with homemade olive oil, fresh basil, tomatoes, and buffalo mozzarella. Worried there was not nearly enough food, she took out some figs whose purple color complimented the sunflower arrangements on the table. Other fruits, grapes, watermelon, cantaloupe, strawberries, and cherries were arranged on the table next to the *cannolis, sfogliatelle*, napoleons, ricotta pie, and other baked goods Liliana had brought home from the bakery. Amara had warned her daughter about bringing so many cream-filled pastries, but Liliana ignored her mother. She rarely disobeyed her or ignored her advice. Amara didn't want to be embarrassed in front of the village because of her daughter's decision to rebel—a behavior she expected out of Angela. Liliana knew better than to serve food like the sfogliatelle, whose cream would soften the crisp outer shell. Amara surveyed the table. Satisfied, she reached into her apron and took out the letter intended for Liliana.

30 March 1953

My Dearest Liliana,

It has been three years since I last saw you covered in flour at the bakery. Do you remember what we discussed the last day I saw you and we stood with the counter between us? I think every day about how I asked you to join me in Venezuela when I was established. Liliana, I have been working making shoes here in Valencia so we can be together. I wake up every morning, look out at the ocean that separates us, and think about how I need you here. Liliana, I have money now and am successful, so different from when I lived in Italy. I can finally look past all those years my family suffered because of poverty and war.

People tell me to find a young woman here, then I will be truly happy and settled, but I have already found my woman. Come here and be my wife. We can live full lives here. Valencia is nothing like Gildone, hidden in the mountains away from the city and water. In Valencia, you can be free, not trapped by the stone, our families, and the people.

Liliana, here we can visit the ocean every day.

Please, be my wife.

You could have your own bakery and together we could give the Italians here a little bit of home. Giovanni San Michele, you know him from church, tells me how much he misses going to the Farinacci Bakery to get sfogliatelle. Just the other day he was telling me how he's never had a millefoglie as good as the ones he had at the Farinacci bakery. I instead miss your sofgliatelle. I also miss seeing you take a bite and getting sugar all over your face.

I picture your hair pulled up in the bakery and your dirty apron. Liliana, I miss seeing you wipe your face and accidentally wiping flour on your forehead. I have been waiting for you, Liliana. I have waited for over two years, and I need you to be with me.

Liliana, every day I think about how you told me you'd wait for me while I got settled in Venezuela. I think only of you.

It has been difficult to correspond with you, especially since I am not sure if my letters are arriving. I have sent many letters since I arrived and have received no response; still, I wait. Liliana, I need you here. I will wait impatiently for you to arrive. Enclosed is money for your trip. Until then, I love you.

With all my love I wait,
Raffaele

Amara stood in the kitchen reading the letter. Her eyes narrowed as she looked at Raffaele's scribbles. Of course, this would arrive today, of all days. She took a deep breath, softening the wrinkles on her face only to have them return as she frowned. Amara put her hands on the kitchen table and bowed her head down. She filled her lungs with air and rolled her eyes back. She heard her daughter coming down the stairs and pocketed the letter, choosing to deal with its disposal later. Liliana did not need to know of its existence. Its obvious signs of neglect by the postal workers in Miami and Rome were a sign. Raffaele was of no importance anymore to the Farinacci family.

Part I: LILIANA

Chapter 1

She arrived at her parents' doorstep after a day at the bakery. She usually went straight home to prepare dinner, but he could wait to eat, just like she would have to wait for him to call for her. Every day she would leave for the bakery while the sun was still resting behind the mountains. The sky a deep black. The stars getting in their last twinkles before first light. She'd peck Domenico on the cheek who didn't have to be up for a few more hours. He'd grunt a kiss at her and roll over to the center of the bed. When she returned from the bakery for dinner, she always found him sitting on the patio with a cigar and a glass of her father's wine. He'd ask "What's for dinner?" and she'd breath in the thick air as she settled into the kitchen to prepare their food.

Liliana knocked on the door, then crossed her arms and waited. She hoped her father would answer, but instead, her mother opened the door.

"Come in. I just made some espresso."

"I don't want espresso." The smell of the coffee made her nauseous. Still, she let Amara poured her a coffee as they sat on the balcony table that overlooked her mother's immaculate garden.

"Tell me."

Liliana was unsure how to begin. Her mother had tolerated a lot from her daughters, and she would have to deal with more.

"He's leaving for Venezuela." Liliana took a deep breath, "He told me last night. I hadn't even finished setting the table, and there he was standing in the kitchen doorway telling me. He is going to leave in a month."

"Are you going with him?"

"He said he'll call for me when he's settled." She said it again silently trying to convince herself.

Amara had heard this same story years ago from her mother, Agostina.

Before Amara was old enough to remember her father, Dante took a job in Venezuela. Amara could not recall missing her father but was sure it had happened. He was asked to head a construction project that would take three years. The money was good, and they would be provided for. This was needed desperately since there had not been work since 1920, the Great War was over, and they were beginning to suffer. Agostina traveled with Dante to Naples to see him off. She watched as her husband marched to the deck and waved. As the ship pulled out of the dock, his face blended into those faces of the other men waving to their wives.

Four years passed.

She hadn't heard from Dante, except through money that arrived every three months. He had not sent a letter or a telegram— only cash. Agostina hadn't heard his voice or seen his writing in four years. She remembered his face only like the one in the photograph on the fireplace mantle. The photo was of Dante as a young man. He wore boots to his knees and a flat top hat. He had few medals since the photo was taken at the beginning of his military career. He smiled, with a clean face not knowing the terror he would soon see; his skin clean, shaved, and fresh. Agostina told Amara how she would stare and stare at the photo, trying to remember how he looked when he frowned or smoked his pipe, but couldn't.

Amara remembered the day her mother began packing. Agostina only packed the essentials, all of which fit into a small sage suitcase. She kept saying, as her daughter watched her fling items into the hard, plastic square, "I won't be long. Don't you worry, carina. I won't be long." Amara remembered how her mother placed the packed suitcase at the entrance of the house. It stayed there, packed, for almost a month. Amara could not remember the exact day or precise time her mother left, but she did know that it happened. She was left with her aunt for a month, maybe three. Time is difficult for children to gauge. When Agostina returned, it was with Dante. She explained years later what happened.

"Your father, Amara, is a pig." She stopped as if catching herself. "But you know those Venezuelan women make themselves available. And they are beautiful, Amara; the most beautiful women in the world. It would be difficult for any man to resist. This is why men need wives. We protect them from themselves. I had to go and find him. I love him, and I believe he loves me, but that wet sea air fogged his mind."

As a child, Amara didn't understand, but as she watched many women in Gildone have their hearts cast into the Mediterranean, she understood. There had been many men who left Italy, Amara remembered. For a time, it seemed Gildone had no men, all of them overseas, stuck in foreign places, and after the war, they attempted an escape. What puzzled Agostina, and later Amara, was that the men who left for Brazil and Argentina called for their wives or returned; it was Venezuela where they lost themselves. Many Gildonese men were remembered for the last time as a fading face waving on a ship.

Amara looked at her daughter, who had stopped speaking and was now barely sipping on her espresso. She was tempted to tell Liliana about how her grandmother had been so courageous many years ago, but she resisted. Amara worried that her daughter would think of Raffaele, whose face she had surely not forgotten. There was no need to upset Liliana further. Instead, she placed her hands on her daughter's shoulder. "Don't worry. You'll be fine."

This was the best Amara could do. Telling her daughter about Agostina would have worried her even more. No wife should wonder, as her husband departed, if he too would be tempted by the beautiful women, the ocean, and humid air. These were thoughts of wives who had cooked too many kilos of pasta and spent years sleeping back to back with their husbands, both forgetting why they married in the first place.

"I will be fine. I think I'm just surprised." Liliana stood, remembering Domenico would arrive home soon, and she still hadn't started dinner. She had even forgotten the fresh bread and thought about walking back to the bakery to get some. She would serve dinner without fresh bread.

She returned, finding Domenico in his usual spot drinking wine and smoking a cigar, listening to the radio. She entered the kitchen and began preparing supper. She could feel his presence behind her.

"What are we having?"

"Rabbit with veggies and polenta."

"Oh." She could hear him shuffle his feet.

"It will be ready soon." She hoped he understood she didn't want to discuss his rash decision.

As she placed the food on the table, he reached for the bread. He sat looking at the bread and broke off a piece and winced as he ate it. Though bread was her business, she could not understand what was so special about fresh bread. It had sat out for one day. This didn't make it taste terrible. She liked to place it in the wood oven and crisp the edges again. The crunch of the crust was revived, giving the day-old bread a second chance. The inside regained its chewy consistency, a perfect contrast to the crust.

"Is it so hard to remember the bread?"

Liliana looked up. She said nothing.

"Well, the rabbit is good." He grunted. She remembered how much he liked this meal the first time she made it for him. Rosemary had a way of making everything taste better. She had minced the rosemary, garlic, parsley, and oregano and marinated the rabbit with the herbs and generously salted it. The olive oil helped prevent the rabbit from drying out, so did a generous pour of white wine. Even after a long day of standing in the bakery and braiding bread, Liliana found pleasure in cooking for her husband. This was how she showed him she loved him.

She thought back to her conversation with her mother about him leaving and hoped that one of these days she'd make him the perfect dish to hold him here in Gildone.

"Thank you." He wasn't one to give compliments. She smiled at him. "It was nice today," She continued, "and the bakery was so busy. The day went by so quickly."

"That's good." His eyes never looking up from his plate.

"How was work?" She asked not really caring about his answer. She was only thinking about his upcoming departure.

"You how it is getting ready for the harvest. We have to make sure the trees are happy." He continued talking about the olive trees. "There are so many of us out there on the fields. I don't know how senore Michele can afford to pay us all."

"Well, he is going to pay you, right?"

"I think so. There are some days when I miss the work from the war." His voice quieted.

Liliana hadn't known him during the war. They met shortly after he came back. Everything was bad after the war. The fields had been ignored while the men fought.

"What do you mean?"

"I just thought after the fighting ended I was going to be able to serve as a police commander or something. Instead, I'm shaking trees so it will rain olives."

Instead of letting him continue, Liliana interrupted him as she cut her food with a violent stab of her knife which screeched across her plate. She was waiting for him to explain, once again why he needed to go away. It was her fault for bringing it up.

She looked up at him, raising her eyebrows and pursing her lips. Her eyes returned to her plate. She wasn't sure what to say. She imagined a different type of dinner where they sat next to each other, not across from each other. Her foot would nudge his under the table. They'd look up from their plates staring as if intoxicated by each other. She's raised her eyebrow at him and smiled a secret at him. He's put his hand gently on her wrist. It would look like a quiet scene from a Humphrey Bogart movie.

Instead, the sounds coming from their kitchen were of forks hitting antique ceramic plates and the ripping of warm bread. Neither of them spoke now. Liliana had nothing to say. He was going to do whatever he wanted to, nothing she could say would stop him.

"Are you not going to speak to me?" he asked. His voice was stuck in the back of his throat and what was usually a booming voice sounded small and weak.

She looked up.

She opened her mouth to speak, but the words were caught behind her teeth. She took a breath.

"I just wish you didn't have to leave." She paused. "Are things so terrible that you have to go?" She stopped before saying she loved him, she wasn't sure what stopped her but the words seemed to not want to escape.

He exhaled a big, long breath. "Listen, I'm doing this for us." He stared with his dark eyes.

"I just think it would be better if you stayed. We just got married, for crying out loud. Shouldn't we enjoy this time together? The bakery is doing well..." Her voice trailed off. She'd made these points before with no success.

"Lili, there is no work for me here. The money is good down there." How many wives had heard this before? How many were left seeing their husband's handwriting on an envelope with no message and some cash?

She nodded. What else could she say? He'd already made up his mind.

"I'm sorry about the bread. It slipped my mind." She retrieved the empty plates, bringing them to the kitchen sink. She turned the water on. Domenico finished his meal to the sound of plates clinking. He got up, and left his plate on the table. After cleaning up, she headed for the bedroom. It had been a long day. She retrieved her prayer books, got into the sheets, and sat in bed.

Seeing she had retired upstairs, Domenico joined her. The tension followed him from the kitchen. Liliana sat on the bed which faced the door and didn't look up at him when he entered, turning her face away from him so he couldn't see her eyes watering. She could feel him looking at her, but sat motionless as if the air in the room were stiff. He said nothing to her as he hit lit a cigarette. While the two of them had argued in the short time they had been married, it had been about trivial things: the placement of furniture or the fresh bread. Liliana watched her mother pick her battles. She often witnessed her father win arguments with her mother—well, he thought he'd won, having gotten his way. Nevertheless, Liliana was well aware that her mother was the commander of the family. Her father's minor victories were meaningless compared to the control she had over the family. Her mother was the one who had decided that Raffaele wasn't good enough for her. Amara decided to have

Domenico introduced to her. Amara *strongly* encouraged Liliana to be open to the idea of marrying Domenico.

When they met for the first time, Liliana remembered being nervous. Her thoughts were consumed by Raffaele and now her family was introducing her to this new man. Domenico was breathlessly handsome. He had a perfect head of black wavy hair and a strong jaw that looked like it could crush steel. His eyes were round and a deep, almost-black. He stood as if he knew he was handsome, teetering between confident and cocky. She recalled looking at his dark lashes and wondering how often his lashes got caught in his eyes. His voice was a low baritone which made it hard for him to whisper. The few times they'd taken chaperoned walks, he tried speaking softly and Liliana shivered, feeling his breath in her ear and traveling down her shoulder. He was also quiet and stoic, so Liliana could never tell what Domenico was thinking, making him difficult to read. Anyone would have said he was handsome. He could have been a movie star, why was he being introduced to her? How could she marry someone like him, quiet, handsome, soon-to-be successful? The flutter of excitement she once felt for Raffaele appeared to be present with Domenico. Raffaele leaving had changed everything. Things were different when he was the one she thought about spending her forever with.

Months before Raffaele left for Venezuela, Liliana was walking through town headed toward via Farinacci. The sun was starting to set, and the breeze was a reminder of how summer was fleeting. Raffaele stood in one corner of the piazza, knowing this was the time she walked home. As she crossed the center of the square, he would rush to cross her path as if trying to crash into her. Liliana would always stop just before bumping into him. She could walk this path blind, knowing exactly which cobblestone to stop at.

"Every day, we do this song and dance, Lili."

Her hands moved toward her hair in a gentle sweep. She could do this with him forever.

"Every day," she'd repeat with a smile. He would then take her hand in his and place his other hand on her waist. This big show of affection in the center of town for everyone to see would then make her nervous. She'd straighten her apron with her free hand, flour would dust her shoes, and she'd pull away from him knowing they'd continue this the next day. Then he left her.

Left her to wait.

Domenico was traditionally handsome, easy to desire. He looked like a provider, but he didn't make her smile the way Raffaele did. When Liliana married, her mother reminded her that beneath their strong masculine exteriors, husbands were well aware that their wives were in control. Liliana looked up from her prayer books to Domenico, whose tan muscular arms were crossed over his chest as he lay down, breathing deep, almost asleep. She wondered if her mother was right. Domenico didn't seem aware of her wifely power, but she was confident he'd figure it out soon enough.

Liliana finished her rosary, returning it to the painted wood trinket box resting on her nightstand. She reached for her lamp, turned the switch, and brought part of the room into darkness. She lay on her side, her back to her husband. He rested his hand on her shoulder. Her eyes became heavy, and as she drifted away, she decided she would forgive him in the morning.

Chapter 2

The month passed quickly and Domenico was set to leave. Liliana packed the bag herself, making sure he had everything he would need. In a leather folder, she prepared his documents and slipped a photo of the two of them from their wedding into his passport. She closed the bakery in order to see him off even though her father had offered to take over for the hour she would be gone. She watched him and he watched for the bus. Liliana noticed his hands had a slight quiver. He looked back her then darted his gaze back to where the bus would park. His dark eyes looked hungry, eager to succeed, she thought.

He fiddled with his one bag. One. One indication that he would, in fact, return. He couldn't survive with only the one bag. He'd be back.

Liliana looked around and saw many of the townspeople rapt in their day. Senore Dillilo was clearing the coffee cups off the counter at the bar. Louisella was crossing through the piazza holding her son's hand. Her two older children walked behind her. The sun was making its way to its afternoon position. It was going to be hot today, and though fall approached, the daytime's summer heat made her nauseous.

Domenico stood next to some of the other young Gildonese men who had been offered work and opportunity overseas. Some of the men still too young to be married waited with their mothers. The women stood in a circle whispering.

"Guiseppe de Luca left three years ago today, and where is he now? His mother hasn't heard from in almost a year."

"And Paulo and Lucio have both been gone almost four years, and neither of their wives knows where they are."

"Domenica told me she was thinking of heading over there herself to find Francesco."

"Oh, now that's ridiculous."

"Sure, but what is she supposed to do, just wait forever?"

Liliana listened as they listed man after man who had left for Venezuela and was yet to be heard from. Heat rose to her face. When she looked up, Senora Pollentino turned to Liliana and asked about Raffaele.

"Liliana, is Raffaele still over in Venezuela? It seems he left for Venezuela ages ago." The Senora's eyebrows arched upward toward her widow's peak as she said "ages."

Liliana nodded. Yes, he was still gone.

She thought often of Raffaele. He had been gone for nearly three years. She had waited and waited for a letter, just one. A note that implied he hadn't forgotten about her and her promise to wait for him. She often wondered when he would send that all-important letter asking her to join in him Venezuela. She had even been secretly saving money to pay for the ticket. How many times had she begun to write to him? In the years before Domenico, she had thought about leaving and going to Valencia. Surely she'd find him. She could start over, leave the stone roads and mountains of Gildone. But he hadn't called for. He hadn't written. She imagined him standing on the sand, facing the water, a woman with olive skin and long black wavy hair, a siren, one of many, for whom he now made beautiful shoes. She took in a long breath of air, hoping that as she exhaled, she could push down the tears that were beginning to form. She wished Senora Pollentino would desist.

The bus would take Domenico and the others to Naples, where they would board a ship. Families would stand on the marina, waving to loved ones, tears clinging to their cheeks. If the stories were true, the ship would turn back to Italy, the promise of opportunity sounding from the horn, returning to retrieve another batch of Italian husbands for Venezuela. There the South American heat would engulf them; the sexy women seduce them; husbands forgetting their wives, boys forgetting their mothers.

#

10 July 1950

Dear Liliana,

The trip overseas is finally over. Spending a month on this boat has made me restless. I missed working with my hands and my workshop. You know how much I love making shoes.

There were some nights when the ocean was quite violent, and many of us were sick. About halfway through the trip, we were forced to go right through a storm. I could see lightning hitting the ocean next to us. It was terrifying. Still, we managed to get here safely. Now the work can begin. I've made some connections while traveling, and I don't think it will take me very long to get settled. Know that the moment things are ready, I will send for you.

I can't wait to see you again, and here, no less. We will be very happy here. I can tell. Liliana, it's just so beautiful here. I knew I would love it when I saw how the mountains meet the ocean.

With all my love,
Raffaele

Chapter 3

The first night she slept alone was a restless one. She remembered her struggles of adjusting to his presence, and now she adjusted once more. She was never a good sleeper and could not remember if she had ever slept through the night. As children, she and her sister, Angela, fought for territory and bed sheets. Although she and Domenico were more civil about the space on the bed they shared, she had definitely kicked him too many times. She tossed and turned, adjusting to his body heat, heavy breathing, and twitches. She imagined the two of them ten years into their marriage. Liliana would toss and turn, and Domenico, having finally had enough, would push her off the bed, muttering "Enough." After somewhat learning to share the bed, she was forced to adapt to his absence. She rested on her side, hardly displacing the bed sheets where he had slept the night before. Her eyes were heavy from her crying. She was tired most nights but woke often, not from being startled or for her bladder, just awake.

Liliana looked over at Domenico's nightstand. His cigarettes rested next to the lamp. The box was half empty. She took one, lit it, and for the first time in her young life, smoked a cigarette. She sat up in bed, inhaling and coughing. She didn't look graceful or elegant smoking. Instead, with each inhalation, she hunched over coughing, wondering why she didn't stop. The smoke filled the room with a familiar smell. The heat dissipated into her body, the vapor engulfing her. When Domenico smoked, his breathing appeared easier. The orange ash, a dim light near his face, soothed him. He never coughed or struggled. Instead, he had a cool Sinatra-like presence. She finished the cigarette, putting it out in the heavy stone ashtray that rested next to Domenico's lamp.

Deciding she was thirsty, she got up and walked down the stairs barefoot. The heat from her body pushed out through her toes onto the cold tile. She shivered, pouring herself a glass of water. Without hesitation, she turned into the sink and threw up. After the kitchen was clean, she returned to the bedroom; the smell of smoke filled the room. She inhaled Domenico's scent and slept.

#

He had been gone for three weeks. The wind now stronger, colder, blew through the stone walls of Gildone. The cold fall air brought darker mornings, lulling Liliana to sleep late. She noticed more symptoms of the baby growing inside her. For weeks, she denied it. With Domenico being gone and his return unclear, she thought a pregnancy to be unfair. Still, her blouses seemed tighter around her chest. One Sunday, on her way to mass, the buttons on her dress were fighting to escape the buttonholes. Her mother cautioned her against eating too much at work.

"You don't want to have to remake *all* of your dresses, do you?"

Liliana nodded at her mother, unaware.

In the afternoon, after hours of standing and the heat from the oven, she was overcome by fatigue. Her legs felt as though walking through dough, her eyelids heavy. She'd even closed the bakery a couple of times to nap. The closures had not gone unnoticed.

"Lili, Senora Pollentina told me you closed the bakery the other day. She said it was the second time she'd gone there around two, only to find it closed up. Is everything okay?" Angela was concerned. Her sister had a gentleness about her. Her hair was highlighted with strands of gold, even in winter when the sun couldn't work its magic. Even though she was younger than Liliana, the wrinkles around her eyes made Angela seem sage. It was as though Angela had packed more years into her younger life. She had four children now. She had been pregnant and nursing during the first five years of their marriage. This had definitely aged her. Having children had given her a wisdom that Liliana appreciated. Though they had often been pitted against each other in school and by their mother, they were still close. Liliana could always go to Angela for advice. When she and Domenico had started to see each other more often, she found herself spending more time with her sister, asking her about men.

"Angela, should I wear this?" She'd ask before a date with Domenico. "What if he wants to kiss me? What should I do? I don't want him to think I'm loose."

"You don't have to worry about that," Angela would reassure her, laughing. "No, one thinks that about you." This was true. For as long as Liliana could remember, she'd always been the hard worker, the "smart one." Liliana knew this meant she was the one who was compliant. She wasn't rebellious in the same way her sister was. Angela was always the "beautiful one," the one that their father had to "worry about." Her skin was almost the color of sage leaves. When she spent time in the sun, her skin turned a dark like a roasted chestnut. Angela's eyes were like over-sized black olives. Angela's face was dewy, and her figure more feminine. Liliana had golden-brown hair and eyes the color of toast. She was also much thicker than her sister, and her family and the town never neglected an opportunity to remind Liliana of how beautiful her sister was.

She once overheard Senora Pollentina outside of mass tell another woman that once Angela married Gianni, Liliana would finally have a chance at a husband. "Who would choose the chubby, dark one, when they could have the pretty one?"

Regardless of all the competition between the two of them, Liliana was glad to have her younger sister looking after her.

"Senora Pollentina always seems to find it her duty to report on what's going on with everyone in this town." Liliana was frustrated by the Senora's making public the few closures to her sister. Liliana knew Angela would just worry. "I'm fine. I've just been so tired."

Liliana had closed the bakery a few times in the afternoon when she found espresso was no longer the jolt she needed, the dark creamy smell no longer appealing; now it was a source for queasiness. Her mother claimed when she was pregnant, the smell of the espresso beans made her sick. This surprised Liliana since her mother only drank coffee and wine. She wondered if it were possible that she be pregnant.

It was a warm in the back of the bakery. The ovens were firing, and she had several loaves of bread baking. The sweet, yeasty smell was overpowering. She had two more loaves left to braid and bake. She put her hands into the flour and spread it onto the work table. She worked the dough, pulling it apart to make determine when it was time to let it rest. After setting aside to prove, she washed her hands and turned on the radio. *Madam Butterfly* was playing again. Liliana let the music waft in the air, intermingling with the small of the bread. The music was moving, she found herself in tears. She knew.

The morning sun shone; pretending to heat the town. Liliana opened the heavy bakery door. She worked through the morning. Tray after tray of cookies and racks of bread were baked and displayed, and if asked, Liliana would have had no recollection of any of it. The fall air was slightly warmer, darkening the crisping leaves on the trees. She didn't notice Angela enter the bakery near noon. Liliana worked in the back on some *mostaccioli*, prepping the nuts and spices. Angela tapped her shoulder, returning her mind to the bakery.

"Mamma sent me to check on you."

"I'm fine." Those afternoon closures were a rash idea. "I'm just so tired."

The door opened, signaling the beginning of the evening rush.

The sisters spent the dinner rush in a quiet togetherness. Angela helped her with some of the cleanup then attempted to leave. Liliana stalled her and finally spit it out.

"Angela, I think I'm pregnant." Hearing herself say it made it seem real. Angela stopped with the bakery door almost in reach.

"But how? He's been gone for almost a month."

"It must have happened before he left." When else could it have happened? Surely, it wasn't an immaculate conception. "I haven't had coffee in days. The smell of it makes me sick. I also can't remember the last time, well, I—you know."

Angela took Liliana's hand, pressing it into hers.

"I remember hating coffee. Oh, and the crying…"

"He doesn't know, Angela."

"Well, why would he?"

Liliana looked up from the rack of sesame seed bread. She shrugged her shoulders and continued arranging the bread. She was certainly not ready to be a mother. Sure, other women her age were having babies, some already with several, but at twenty-six, what did she know about being a mother? Though she wasn't completely sure about the pregnancy, every day it seemed clearer.

She moved the bread from rack to rack, making room for a fresh batch. As she looked at the rack of bread she remembered a strange dream she'd kept having. She was on a braided loaf of bread that had turned into a ship. She felt safe on the golden-brown loaf and noticed passengers sitting between the different layers of the braid. She was seated next to Domenico. The ship began to rock back and forth and water sprayed her face and her hair was wet from the water. The water grew violent and waves smashed against the bread-boat. She tried to hold on and looked to Domenico for help but as she turned to see him, thinking he would be beside her, she saw he was getting ready to jump off the ship. He looked back at her and shrugged his shoulders before diving, head-first, into the wild sea. The storm strengthened and Liliana found herself alone on the ship. When a large wave smashed into the ship forcing it to flip. Liliana saw herself surrounded by water. The water was warm and a soft cerulean. She could see her dark hair flowing around her face. She looked up and saw the boat floating away. She wasn't worried. She was safe in the water, and she left the feeling of calm wash over her.

"You are going to tell him?"

"Of course." She knew what she would say. She only had to write and send it. By the time she received his response, she'd probably be showing.

"If you need me, you know where to find me." Angela reminded her sister. Liliana packed her sister two loaves of bread and a bag of two biscotti for Angela's children. "You're always spoiling them."

"So, I'm their aunt. I'm supposed to."

"Well, then I'm going to spoil yours."

Liliana looked away from Angela then smiled. If she were pregnant, Angela and her mother would help her. They'd come together as they always did to protect each other.

"Good, because I won't be able to on my own." Liliana's throat was now tense and sore as she tried to hold back tears.

"Oh, stop."

"Honestly, you of all people should know how hard it is to raise a baby alone, especially in this town."

"Sure, but at least you're married." Angela made a good point. She wasn't married when she got pregnant with Giacomo. Liliana was grateful they could be so frank without hurting each other's feelings.

"Angela, I keep thinking about how it was when you were pregnant with Giacomo. I'm not strong like you." One of the things Liliana admired most about Angela was the way she was able to ignore the clucking. Sure, Liliana had seen her sister crying and knew it was hard on her, especially when Roberto's mother wouldn't let him anything to do with his own son, but Angela made coping with that scandal look as simple as turning the other direction and averting the eyes. Angela has even managed to stay on their mother's good side. Though, as Liliana thought about it was more like putting a loaf of bread in the oven and forgetting it was there and smelling it burn.

"You're stronger than you think." Angela looked up then back at her sister, measuring her words. "When it comes time to deal with all the gossip, the fear, or whatever other storm God puts on your path, you find a way. You find a way because you have to. You have to do it for the baby."

"I guess. Still, what if Domenico turns out like all those other men who leave and never come back?"

"Don't say that. It won't happen." Angela's voice was unsure.

"How do you know?"

"I don't, but I do know that everything will be fine." She paused, letting her words sink in. "When I got pregnant with Giacomo, things were different. I was younger than you are now, and Roberto and I were stupid. It didn't help that his mother…" She sighed, reliving the turmoil. "Well, you know the story. I'm just lucky that Gianni was able to see past my stupidity and love

Giacomo as his own. Lili, you'll be fine. I'm sure as soon as Domenico knows you're going to have a baby, he'll rush back over."

"You don't know that." Liliana thought about how she'd told Raffaele she'd wait, and he'd left along with so many others. Only a few of them made it back to this place.

"I do know that the kids, especially Giacomo, are going to love these cookies." Angela hated talking in what-ifs.

"Well, here." Liliana handed her the little brown bag with the cookies and changed the subject. "Give him a kiss for me."

"You want me to stay for a bit longer?"

"No, I just have a few small things to do, then I'll head over to the house."

Angela nodded, leaving her sister alone in the bakery.

#

After whipping the *crema fresca* and adding sugar, lemon, and vanilla oil essence, Liliana indulged in the crisp filo dough pastry. She refrigerated the cream, then packed a pastry for herself. She'd need something sweet after her lonely dinner.

Cooking for one never appealed to Liliana. It was too much work for only one person to enjoy. The mindless work of cooking somewhat soothed her. Liliana prepared the lemon chicken, listening to her favorite radio show. She loved the soap operas, the drama, and scandal. Her sister teased her for liking them. The last of the summer lemon crop had arrived at the market, and she had purchased just enough to make the chicken dish. Her mother's lemon chicken could compete in international cooking competitions. And though she had watched Amara make the dish, she couldn't get the taste quite right. Instead of sautéing the chicken, sometimes Amara stuffed the chicken with lemons and, while it baked, turned it upside down. Liliana could never remember why her mother did this. It was the hand she lacked. Liliana sliced the lemons into circles. As she did this, the butter and oil were heated on the stove. Cutting the onions only aggravated her despair. She poured herself a glass of her father's wine. She thought about how she would have to write Domenico a letter convincing enough to encourage him to return. He was stubborn, and she hated this about him. Though she and Domenico didn't share many traits, her father reminded her, on a regular basis, how she too, was like a mule. What kinds of jobs could there be in Venezuela, out there, in what she imagined to be mountains and jungle, more wilderness than she could ever be comfortable in?

She sautéed the onions, and a roux formed as the onions and butter combined to make the beginnings of a creamy sauce. Liliana took some of her father's white wine and poured it into the butter, onion, and oil mixture. The wine quieted the sizzle of the cooking. She listened to the radio blasting the news: the economy was finally starting to recover.

It had taken nearly a decade. The war had come and gone; still, the Italians down south struggled to find jobs. She added the chicken, one from out back. De-feathering and butchering it had, for the first time, made her queasy. As her finger grazed the chicken's prickly skin, she dry-heaved. It was a relief to put the meat in the pan. As the chicken began to brown, she added the lemon juice and lemons. When she was really in the mood to cook, she would batter the chicken, but this evening, she wanted to hurry up and eat. She placed the chicken on one side of the plate, then added a side of mushrooms, a blend of fall and summer on one plate. Liliana wrapped up the rest of the food, enough for four; she'd never get used to cooking for one.

She cleaned up her dinner plates and sat down at the kitchen table: pen, paper, and pastry in front of her. She took a bite from the fresh millefoglie.

Dearest Domenico,

I haven't heard from you in many weeks. It's been nearly two months since you left. How are you settling in? I hope you're busy with work. I know that's important to you.

Good news! We are going to have a baby. I haven't confirmed it with the doctor yet, but all the signs are there. I'm always hungry, cry just because the wind blows, and just like Mamma and Angela, the smell of espresso makes me ill. I've even been sleeping in later and later, and it's not because of the cold winter ahead. Can you believe it? "A woman knows," my mother tells me, and I just know.

Caro, I really need you to return. If you're worried about work, don't; the bakery is doing well, and I'm sure you've heard Italy isn't in as hard of times anymore. I'm sure you could find work in Campobasso.

Please, come home. The baby and I need you. Domenico, I know I can't do this without you.

I miss you.

Your wife,
Liliana

p.s. Write soon.

She double-checked the address, took the last indulgent bite from the pastry, and sealed the envelope. She pressed the envelope between her rough hands, wishing the letter luck.

At the bakery, she felt better. She could picture Domenico's charming dimples engaged, smiling as he received the news. It would be a good enough reason for him to come home. He was going to have a family now.

She wouldn't be sleeping alone for long. Before they were married, he had mentioned how eager he was to have a child. Although Liliana was sure the making aspect of the process excited him too. He often mentioned how he had wanted siblings growing up, his mother only able to have him. It was rare for a family to have one child, and it was obvious to Liliana that this bothered Domenico. He had grown up with his cousins but having cousins was not the same as having siblings of one's own. It pleased her to know Domenico wanted more than one child. She hoped for a large family. She loved having a sister and brother growing up. She had enjoyed the laughter and the tears that came with having siblings. Her parents, too, came from large families, both the youngest of five. Liliana was always around her siblings and cousins. She loved how boisterous gatherings were and all the shared meals. She wanted this with Domenico.

She wondered what type of father Domenico be. She pictured him arriving home from work doing whatever men did with their sons. She imagined Domenico as a great father to sons. His being so masculine and charming—the way she envisioned sons of hers to be. She would be relieved if she and Domenico were to have sons. Sons were easier; everyone said so. Domenico was sure to be a strict father with girls, not as easygoing as her father. Senore Farinacci had a more nonchalant approach to parenting, which may have been part of Angela's trouble, something the women in town would never let anyone forget.

Domenico was very clear in his likes and dislikes, never wavering on his feelings for her. Liliana liked this about him. He knew what he wanted and went after it. She smiled thinking of how he'd likely open her letter and be excited to return to her, in time to see his firstborn. She smiled thinking of this as she dusted the last of the loaves of bread with flour, placing them into the large wood oven. She looked out at the storefront remembering how simple things were before the men started to leave.

After a couple of months of him courting her, she and Domenico took a long walk along the road that led out of Gildone. They started walking through the town and worked their way up a hill that left Gildone behind them. It was a Sunday afternoon, and the bakery was closed. Amara pushed Liliana out of the door when Domenico arrived to see her.

"Go, go for a walk."

As they walked, Domenico's hand reached for hers.

"I like you, Lili." He was never one to mince words.

She looked down, unsure of what to say to him. She liked him too, but she still had Raffaele on her mind. He'd been gone for about a year, and she still had not received one letter. Meanwhile, Domenico stood next to her. He was strong and handsome. His dark, curly hair always neat and styled. She liked how serious he was. She could see herself being protected by him and not needing anyone else.

"I like you too." Her words, quiet, as if slipping through the wind.

"Lili, I think about the future a lot, and I think you're going to be an excellent mother someday. I want to be there when it happens." He loved talking about the future. He was ambitious. She liked this about him. He was always sharing his dreams with her. As they walked up the hillside, Gildone looked so small. "I can't wait to come home to you and our babies." He said this as if it was set in stone.

Liliana blushed. She liked the idea of babies running around the yard, taking them to the bakery, learning the value of hard work from Domenico. He would make a great father someday.

"I'd like that." She really did. That was the first time, Domenico replaced Raffaele when she thought of the future.

She shook her head to escape her thoughts. She locked the heavy wooden door and headed toward her mother's house. Amara opened the door.

"Espresso?"

"Oh, just the thought of it…"

"So, you are. I had a feeling." The muscles in Amara's face moved into a slight smile, only detectable because the carved wrinkles in her face seemed out of place.

"Yes, I'd like to see the doctor tomorrow to be sure."

Senore Farinacci entered the kitchen, his pipe in hand. He always appeared to be so relaxed. Never a worry on his mind. He was young when he fought in the Great War, only nineteen, but when he came back, the violence he'd seen was assuaged by perfecting pastries and bread. He loved the quiet of the bakery and the wine cellar where he spent hours making wine. He was always easy to find, the smell of his pipe like a signal wafting through the air. He'd passed on his appreciation for silence to Liliana, who worked alongside him in the bakery, rarely speaking as they worked.

"Oh please, take that outside," Amara hissed, staring at the pipe. He placed it on the kitchen counter, walked towards his daughter, and gently placed his hands on her shoulders.

"Why do you need to go to the doctor?"

"Oh, just a check-up."

"Since when…" The women only looked at him.

"Papa, could you watch the bakery?"

"Of course. Angela will help me too. She's about had it with the dress shop."

At that, Amara rolled her eyes.

"Do you need anything else?" she asked Liliana.

"Yes, I better be going. I still need to reheat the lemon chicken for dinner."

#

It would take a week to hear back from the doctor. He would call her when he received the test results. After the initial visit, her fears were beginning to calm. She was glad to have gone in the morning. She stood at the bus stop waiting to head back to Gildone. She would arrive in Gildone just in time to close the bakery. When the bus arrived, she walked to the back and sat so she could look out the window.

The bus would stop in at least four towns before entering Gidone, which rested far up in the mountains. With every stop, Liliana realized how different all the towns were. Even though they looked so close to each other on the maps, they were, instead, quite far away from each other, separated by winding roads and mountainsides. The bus stopped at Domenico's hometown. They were both born on the same side of the mountain, practically *pisanos,* and in many ways, they were cut from the same loaf, still, there was something alien about him. She looked out the window and noticed a group of men standing in the center of the piazza. They stood in a circle laughing. They all had the same dark, slicked-back hair and stone jawlines that she so admired in Domenico, but it was also the middle of the day, and they weren't working. She looked down at her lap. This was why he left to come to Gildone and then left again for Venezuela. A few folks got off the bus and walked toward the men laughing. Liliana watched as they exchanged pleasantries. The bus began to chug forward and move toward Gildone. When they arrived, the center of town was quiet. The men were working out on the fields. She stepped off of the bus. From the center of town, she could see the

39

top of the mountain and the valley below. The buildings around the square made the center feel like a bowl. She thought about how often she and Raffaele had met in the center of town for their daily song and dance. She stood in their spot thinking about how she and Raffaele came from the same batch. She looked back at the bus stop, now empty. The bench near the stop sign inhabited by the old men in town who had seen two wars, drought, and turmoil. They rested with their canes in hand. They sat in silence. She stopped to listen to the wind travel through the leaves of the tree and headed toward the bakery. It was time for her to get back to work.

The following week, the doctor called minutes before she began her walk to the bakery.

The phone rang. She wondered if Domenico would ever call.

"Congratulations, you're going to be a mother." Her hands shook as she held the telephone receiver.

"Thank you, Doctor," her voice quivered as she spoke. She closed the phone line, sat down, and sobbed.

Though the confirmation of her pregnancy was no shock, Liliana walked differently towards the bakery. With each step, she thought of the baby as a secret, even if only for a few minutes. Though tiny, it felt as if the baby was weighing her down.

The door to the bakery seemed heavier than usual as Liliana pulled it towards her. Her father napped in the back, his face relaxed and warmed by the heat from the oven. Liliana looked at her sister and pointed to their father. Angela shrugged her shoulders, smiling.

"So?"

Liliana nodded. Angela rushed from around the counter, hugging her sister.

Senore Farinacci stepped towards them, watching.

"What is all this about?" Angela backed away from her sister. She looked at Liliana with raised eyebrows and pointed her head toward their father.

"You're going to be a grandfather." She blurted it out, like an accidental spill of pastry cream filling.

"Well, that is exciting." He pulled his daughter in for a fatherly embrace. Then he added in an uncomfortable tone, "I think you two have the bakery under control, I'll go home. Can I tell your mother?"

"Yes, although I think she already knows."

"That woman, she knows everything, doesn't she?" He took a big bite of a sfogliatelle and left the bakery, letting the door hit the frame with a bit of a slam.

Chapter 4

Autumn was in full swing before Liliana could even braid a loaf of bread. The valley below Gildone was no longer a hazy green but a rich burgundy, the same shade as homemade wine and pockets of gold. The air was chilled, and she was grateful for the cooler temperatures; the humidity felt as if it had been siphoned out of the air. Her body was unwilling to withstand any heat, especially from the oven. Her belly grew larger and peeked through her clothing. Walking home from the bakery, she noticed the whispers and stares, eyes rolled back as if doing the math. They hadn't started snubbing her, but it was only a matter of trimester. No, she hadn't had an affair, it had happened soon after she and Domenico wed.

Angela knew firsthand how horrible the women were to each other and began walking her sister home. When Angela faced the rumors years before, Liliana appeared indifferent to the looks and gawking, but as Angela's pregnancy was confirmed after months of rumors, she struggled to keep her stoic appearance. At first, Liliana ignored their requests for answers, minding her own business; she kept on. But as Angela's pregnancy became more apparent and Roberto left for God knows where, the women aggressively insulted her sister both to her face and behind her back, whispering *putana* whenever she passed. The town constantly warned Liliana not to behave like her sister, though when the flirtations between she and Raffaele became overt, Liliana became a target for their clucking, making Raffaele's courting a source of both pain and excitement. Angela was forced out of her friendships with the other girls in Gildone, and Liliana, too, was a victim of circumstance.

Gianni's mother was furious he would fall in love with a woman who had gotten pregnant by another man who seemed to vanish.

"Lili, Roberto won't marry me. I don't know where he is. What am I going to do?"

Angela was worried. She was already so pregnant, and Roberto had left Gildone. Angela wrote to him after Giacomo was born, but he never replied. Soon, Angela couldn't find work and was raising her son alone. When Gianni came around, she was only twenty-one. Still young and beautiful. She and Gianni were never apart, and even though Giacomo wasn't his son, he loved him no differently than he would have his own flesh and blood. Gianni's mother would not allow her son to marry Angela. She had power in the town, her husband being the only pharmacist for kilometers. Gianni was learning from his father. He was highly desired, and his mother knew this. There was no way *her* son would marry Angela the whore. The women relished in the gossip and saga of it all and sided with Gianni's mother. It hurt Liliana to see her sister miss out on being settled with Gianni, especially since it appeared they were so good together. It seemed as though, she too, was destined to face the same treatment as her sister.

"Why can't they just mind their own?"

"Because they're old," Angela was quick to respond. "And have nothing better to do."

"They are old. One day we'll be like them clucking in circles. Cheep. Cheep. Cheep."

They giggled, laughing, almost forgetting about all the women and their senseless clucking.

"Angela?" Liliana asked, her voice shook and dropped an octave. She whispered. "I'm so scared."

"I know." Angela held her sister's arm. Even though she was younger, Liliana felt her

sister's motherly wisdom seep through her sweater.

"You know, I haven't heard from him. It's been over three months. Not even a telegram."

"You will. You will."

#

Winter was working its way up the mountain; her belly grew larger. For months, she walked back to the house, opened the mailbox and found nothing of import. On this day, she opened the mailbox as the baby kicked inside her. Kicking hard, wanting to see what was inside the striped envelope Liliana held it tightly in her cold, gloved hands.

Liliana,

How could you be pregnant? I won't be coming back, not for a while. I'll send money when I can. Let me know when the baby comes.

You'll be fine.

Domenico

Enclosed in the envelope: cash wrapped in newspaper. It was a small amount, enough to buy some groceries. She placed her hands on her belly. A tiny little foot tapped her gently. The letter fell from her hands. She bent down, arching her back awkwardly to pick it up. She went inside and placed the letter on a small table in the foyer. She went into the kitchen and sat at the table. She wiped her eyes.

"He is not coming back," Liliana told her sister and mother.

"He'll come when the baby arrives. Stop your worrying," Amara said as she moved about the kitchen putting dishes away.

"He will. Mamma's right."

"I just can't raise this baby by myself. Not with all of Gildone giving me looks, and to make matters worse, did you know his mother wouldn't even speak to me?" Liliana became teary.

"Who cares?" Angela replied.

"She's about to be a grandmother. Her son has produced a child," she barked.

"Well, she was never known for being *sympatica*, even when we were younger."

Amara and Guisepina, Domenico's mother, had gone to school together. Guisepina left Gildone when she married Michele, Domenico's father. They lived just a few towns away, but Amara made it seem as though Guisepina had forgotten where she was from. Amara wouldn't reveal too many details – she was a secretive woman – but Amara did seem to imply that Guisepina was not the sweetest of girls.

Amara watched her daughter sink into a kitchen chair. She continued to tidy the kitchen. She remembered those times when Guisepina had given her a sneer or repeated gossip when they were growing up. She was a miserable woman. Nothing had changed from when they were children.

"Ma, that's not the point. I'm about to raise this baby alone. Me, a baby….and the bakery." Liliana let herself go, shaking as she cried. "And," she breathed in her tears. "And they're all just waiting for me to fail."

Amara looked at her daughter, understanding Liliana's fear. She wouldn't be alone, and she reminded her of this; she had Angela and herself.

"It's going to be okay. You're just feeling wild because of the baby." Amara cut three slices of bread, drizzled them with olive oil and sprinkled them with sugar. She placed the food in front of Liliana.

"Here, eat this. You'll feel better."

Liliana looked up and pushed the food away. The sweet yeasty smell of the bread, sugar, and oil made her smile. This was her favorite childhood snack. Liliana remembered her mother making it for Angela and Guiseppe, her brother, after school. Amara would then push them out to the door and tell them not to come back until the sun was setting. After Guiseppe died, Amara lost whatever softness she had left after the wars. Her brief tenderness was refreshing to the two sisters. Liliana took a slice and inhaled the smell of the bread, oil, and sugar. She closed her eyes and took a bite.

#

5 September 1950

My Dearest Liliana,

Did you get my last letter? I was surprised not to hear from you; you're usually so quick to respond to me. I also miss hearing from you. I wish it wasn't so expensive to call you. Daniele told me he tried calling home a few weeks ago, but the connection was terrible. I wish I could hear the sound of your voice.

I recently moved into a small house with a few other men from Gildone. We are all looking for work. I'm doing some construction work, but once I save up enough, I'll start making shoes again. I just need money for supplies and space to work.

The weather is much nicer now that the rain has quieted. Lili, you've never seen such rain or felt such heat. When the sun comes out, steam rises from the grass. The air is thick enough to slice.

I hope to hear from you soon.

With all my love,
Raffaele

Chapter 5

She walked to the bakery as if led by her belly. Angela escorted her sister each morning after the first ice storm arrived. The valley in fall, a beautiful palate of rich purples and oranges, was now washed away by the snow and ice. Winter had moved in, an unwelcome tenant. Liliana's hillside home provided the ice with a perfect space to rest but created a treacherous slope. Amara, Senore Farinacci, and Angela refused to let Liliana walk through it without assistance.

At first, Angela's morning arrivals annoyed Liliana. She felt capable; she *had* walked on ice before. What difference did the baby make? But as she grew and grew, it appeared her mother and sister were correct; she'd fall and kill herself on that slope.

"You'll freeze to death."

"And no one will find you," Angela added.

Liliana laughed at them.

"Senore Timonare arrives the moment I've pulled the first batch of biscotti out of the oven."

Liliana remembered how Raffaele did this too. He would come in and say, "It's my breakfast. The best start to the day." He'd wink, then walk out of the door backward, stumbling on it. As the pregnancy progressed, she thought of her old boyfriend, missing their afternoon rendezvous. In a different universe, she and Raffaele would have had a satisfying life together. Nearly three years had passed since he left for Venezuela. Had he stayed, she imagined she'd have at least two children with his wavy gold hair and soft green eyes. Maybe one of them would have inherited that sweet dimple on the left side of his cheek, the other his long eyelashes.

"I don't care if he waits for you at the door. Your sister is going to start walking with you." Her father's voice came from upstairs. He lit his pipe and returned to the newspaper. It was final.

#

Each morning, after walking Giacomo to school, Angela arrived wrapped in a dull green scarf tucked into her wool coat. Just as her gloved hand came to rest on the door, Liliana would push herself through it, her coat unbuttoned, neck exposed.

"Are you crazy?"

"What? I'm dying of heat." She looked down at her stomach. Her sweater pushed back against her belly. "It's practically an oven in there. Plus, fresh air is good for the baby."

Angela rolled her eyes, moving her hands towards Liliana's coat in a quick effort to wrap her up. Liliana elected to fabricate facts like this. She noticed as the trimesters passed that she had gotten very good at manifesting medical advice to suit her whims. Although she was sure her sister didn't believe her, she continued to make up facts that went against common sense, always adding, "It's good for the baby." This made it seem like a good idea; whatever it took to inhale the clean winter air. She enjoyed how it pierced through her nostrils, cooling her core.

"Well, I'm not going to parade through the center with you unbuttoned. You know what they'll say, especially Senora Pollentino. Can you imagine?"

Liliana knew the Senora would rush her and button her coat, wrapping the scarf around her neck so tightly it would nearly be murder. She'd then spout off about her daughter's pneumonia, which she never seemed to have recovered from.

"Oh, fine." She buttoned her coat while looking out onto the valley. The winter sun reflected off the snow, reminding Liliana of lemon *50ranite*, a summer's dessert.

Angela helped her with her buttons. Liliana finished adjusting her coat and noticed her shoes were untied. She groaned, annoyed that her belly prevented her from noticing these small details before she stepped out of the house. Angela looked up at her.

"I'll do it." She bent down, head brushing against her future niece or nephew.

"Angela?"

"Yes?"

"Do you remember when Guiseppe taught us to tie our shoes?"

"Huh?" She paused. "Hmm, I haven't thought about that in years."

"Remember that song he sang when he showed us?"

"Uh, huh." She stood up.

"I keep dreaming about him." She stopped. "He wouldn't have let these horrible things happen to us."

"Brothers aren't supposed to." They looked at each other, both remembering how Guiseppe the same green eyes and a toothy smile that scrunched up his nose like their father. They headed into the center, arm in arm, parading through the town like two old ladies, giggling and smiling.

"You two are finally getting along?" Senora Pollentino shouted. Her front balcony served as her lookout. The Senora had inherited the property from her mother, who had also had the reputation of having a nose too large for her face. The Senora staked out the town, making sure she had every ounce of gossip possible. Liliana assumed the Senora interrogated all the passersby, not just them.

"Guess so," Angela replied as they continued working their way to the bakery.

"Every morning she says it," Liliana said in a hushed voice to Angela.

"I know, and if we weren't getting along, she'd say something about that too."

"Hey, Liliana! You're coming far along there. Look at you, I can see your belly through your coat." The sisters looked up. Raffaele's brother, Tonino, walked towards them. He looked like his brother, except with a darker complexion. Having worked in the fields during summer, the color was now permanent. Around his eyes were crow's feet that made his somewhat crooked-tooth smile appear gentler. Seeing Tonino forced a rush of blood to her face. She was hot and cold. A weight pushed onto her chest and she struggled to catch her breath. Without any warning, she remembered a dream from a few nights ago. A man stood in a field of olive trees. His amber-brown hair blew in the breeze. Liliana couldn't decipher his face. The leaves and branches a luxurious silver. She stood far from him, just out of reach. He smiled at her and waved. On the other side of the field, she could see another man, his back turned to her. She turned her attention back to the man waving, but he was gone. She woke up crying. She held onto Angela, unable to stand on her own.

"Hey, look who it is." Angela held her sister up.

"Tonino, how are you?"

They spoke briefly of the pregnancy, the changing weather, and the bakery, all while walking away from each other. Tonino's voice, similar in timbre to his brother's, rang in Liliana's ears. Raffaele and Tonino were always together growing up. Raffaele had fairer skin, but they both shared that same dimple on their left cheek. Less than two years apart, they'd both been sent off to fight during the war, and the town worried their mother would lose both her sons. Everyone was relieved when they returned unharmed. The few times Liliana had seen Tonino in town, she'd been afraid to ask about Raffaele, worried she wouldn't want to hear what he would say. She was grateful not to run into Raffaele's family often. It would only remind her of a happy past and how Raffaele was now so out of reach, the past so different from her situation now. Pregnant and—if Domenico's lack of correspondence indicated anything—alone. She instead always ran into the gossips that were always so kind to point out that her husband was likely to miss the birth of his firstborn child.

"When was the last time you heard from Domenico?" her neighbor asked her as they were leaving mass. "It would be a shame for him to not meet his firstborn." Liliana nodded.

"Did you hear about Roberto, Maria's husband?" Liliana hadn't, but it didn't matter; the way everyone gossiped, she knew the rest of the story was to follow. "Turns out he has a whole new family. Three kids with some woman in Caracas. Can you imagine?" Liliana could. Her face dropped. "Oh goodness. I'm sorry. Have you heard from your husband?" She was never sure how to respond.

"These men," they'd say. "What are you going to do?" Liliana would shrug her shoulders when townspeople would say this to her as if the men abandoning their family was the same as two boys wrestling over a toy. It was all she could do to keep her heart from lurching out of her throat.

She turned back watching as Tonino walked towards the bus stop. He was headed to work in the valley to continue preparing for spring. They entered the dark bakery; Liliana took in a deep starchy breath. Angela turned on the lights. The hum of electricity overpowered Liliana's thoughts.

"Wow, he looks so much like Raffaele." Angela placed her arm on Liliana's shoulder. Liliana looked up at Angela. "I wonder what happened to him?"

Liliana looked away from her sister trying to stall the tears.

More than she wanted to admit. Every day she thought of Raffaele and his daily visits, his exclamations of love for her, and his sweet mischievous eyes. She remembered the gossip, the whispers about Angela and Gianni, and the day her father gently told Liliana how Raffaele did not meet his and Amara's approval, how she could do better than a farmer. She wondered if he had finally opened a business as he had planned. She imagined a small cobbler's shop in the very center of the Venezuelan jungle. He couldn't possibly think of her any longer. They all forgot about home when they breathed in the exotic air. Amara truly believed Liliana had done better with Domenico, the decorated soldier who worked his way up from shaking the olives to managing several farms in the area. She wondered what Raffaele would say if he could see how her life had turned out, so unlike the one he had planned for them. She pictured Raffaele with a Venezuelan goddess planning a new future.

"It's so strange how he just disappeared," Angela continued, pulling Liliana's thoughts away from Venezuela.

"I'm going to start the biscotti." Angela understood and prepared the cash register.

In the back, Liliana prepped for the biscotti. She took out the eggs, flour, almonds, and other ingredients. She cracked the eggs and separated the yolks from the whites, using her fingers as a filter. The ivory slime slipped through her fingers. She rinsed her hands and added the other wet ingredients, inhaling the anise extract, looking forward to its sweet tangy smell as it baked through the biscotti. She beat the wet mixture, hearing the front doorbell ring. She beat the mixture harder.

"Liliana, you know that isn't going to be any good if you keep beating it."

She looked up at her sister.

"What is wrong with you today?"

Liliana put the whisk down and sobbed.

"This baby is going to be here so soon, and the last I heard from Domenico was in the fall. It's nearly March."

"I should have never married him."

Liliana stood taller and placed her hands on her belly. "Look at me—alone, pregnant, and so fat." They heard the front door of the bakery, but no bell. Senora Pollentino had entered the bakery, gently opening the door.

"Excuse me, young ladies, is the bread ready?"

Liliana and Angela walked toward the front counter together.

"Excuse me, Senora Pollentino. What would you like?" Liliana stared hard at the woman, working hard to hold her tongue.

"Oh, the usual."

"Two sesame loaves coming up." She reached for the loaves, her big belly holding her down, getting in the way of the racks. Angela slid her hand gently behind her sister and retrieved them with grace.

"It's so nice to see you two getting along. Not like when you were little. I remember you two always fighting." She paused. "It used to drive your Nonna Agostina mad."

Liliana hadn't thought of her grandmother in a long time. She remembered a tough woman, much like her own mother. Agostina had little tolerance for nonsense. She recalled that her grandmother appeared perpetually annoyed at her grandfather. Nonna Agostina also made the best *pizza minestra*. The crispy cornbread glazed with the perfect amount of olive oil, the bread mashed and mixed with the dark mustard leaves served next to her homemade sausage. Sometimes she would dice tomatoes, adding color to the drab dish. Liliana tried over and over to get the flavors of hers to match her grandmother's but was unable. Tonight, she'd try again.

Angela finished ringing up Senora Pollenito's purchase.

"Your grandmother was a great woman," the Senora continued. "You know that, right?"

"Well, of course." Liliana quipped. Where was the Senora going with this? Liliana sensed an insult ready to slip from the woman's acid mouth.

"You should ask your mother about how strong she was. Your grandmother would walk by the bar, and the men would shake." Senora Polletino walked toward the door. "Just ask your mother." She smirked as she walked out the door onto the ice-covered stone. The Senora never seemed to face the same sagas as her Gildonese neighbors. Her three daughters all married well and she was never of want for anything. In many ways, she was the town historian—she knew the histories of all the families in the small, stone village.

The door closed, and the two sisters looked at each other. Angela reflected Liliana's confused look, but Liliana's gut made her think Angela knew what Senora Pollentino was referring to. She'd ask her mother, though that didn't guarantee she'd get a straight answer.

Leaving Angela to the front counter, Liliana returned to the biscotti. She looked at the wet egg mixture. It had sat for only minutes, but it was obvious this batch was not going to be a good one. The egg whites were flat and yellow again lacking the necessary whip to fold into the yolk mixture. She started again, tasting the dough before shaping it into a log. Deciding it was satisfactory, she sprinkled sliced almonds on the top, an extra she usually reserved for the holidays.

While the biscotti baked, she braided the bread dough and prepared the racks for the lunch rush. The schoolchildren would come to bring bread home for their mothers. Wanting to please the children, she prepared a quick batch of biscotti *brutti ma buoni* cookies for them. The small timer she kept near the oven chimed, warning Liliana to retrieve the biscotti. As she pulled them out, the bell rang on the front door.

"Senore Timonare," she heard Angela say. "She just needs to slice them, and then they'll be ready."

"Good, I could smell them baking." Senore Timonare had retired from the fields after the war, long before Liliana had taken over the bakery. He lived in the building next door. The same air circulated through the ancient building. The smell of Liliana's delicious treats was a potpourri for his home.

Liliana wrapped a half dozen biscotti alongside some *brutti mai buoni* in a box for the senore. Every time she heard the bell ring, she remembered walking to counter, looking up, only to see Raffaele thrusting the door open to rush to the counter.

"It's time for my breakfast. My favorite time of day." He nearly sang the words.

"Good morning, Raffaele." She loved saying each syllable of his name. She would let the "r" roll off of her tongue and linger at the "el-leh,"

"Are the biscotti ready?"

"Yes, I'm waiting for them to cool so I can slice them." He knew this was going to be her answer, but this exchange was a ritual now.

"May I walk you home this evening?" He asked her this every day, and every day she made him wait for an answer. She turned her back to him and walked to the back of the bakery. She turned to see him leaning, his elbows on the counter and his face in hands, a slight smirk on his face. After thinking he had waited long enough, she returned with a tray of biscotti. She'd even put the cafeteria on so they could share some espresso.

"So, may I?" he'd ask again.

"One second, let me get the coffee." She walked away again, this time letting her hips sashay a bit more dramatically.

When she returned with the coffee, she placed two biscotti on a small plate and poured the espresso for the two of them. His elbows remained on the counter as he looked up at her. His long eyelashes reinforced his baby face, and Liliana could see his sweet dimple.

"I'm only going to ask you one more time." His voice flirtatious, yet assertive.

"Yes. Yes, you may walk me home." As if tired from the exchange, Liliana would place her elbows on the counter and face him.

"See you at five-thirty." He would jump up and kiss her cheek just as another customer rang the bell.

The baby kicked, returning Liliana to the bakery where Senore Timonare waited for his biscotti and neither Raffaele nor Domenico were waiting in line behind him. The jungle air had likely consumed Domenico as well, which explained his lack of correspondence with his expecting wife. Liliana debated if she should bother to let him know when the child arrived. She knew her mother and father, as well as his parents, would disapprove of her not telling him—after all, he had played a large role in its conception.

"I added some biscotti brutti for you. I know how much everyone seems to like them."

"*Graci*, carina," He spoke to her belly. "I see you every day, though today you look so much more beautiful than you always do. Doesn't she?" He turned to Angela.

"Your eyes are old, Senore. I look like I do every day—pregnant." She thanked him with her smile and the box of cookies. He returned the smile, his old face grinning at the two sisters.

"*A domani.*"

"Yes, tomorrow."

#

That evening, they left the bakery, and the sun hid behind the mountain, making it easier for the cold winter air to penetrate their clothing. As they walked together, Liliana gently questioned her sister.

"So, Nonna Agostina, what was that about?" Liliana poked her sister.

"I don't know." Angela turned away from Liliana's eyes. "You should ask Mamma."

"I guess I'll have to." She pulled her body away from Angela.

Even though her pregnancy had brought them closer and they finally could agree and discuss motherhood, sex, men, and indulge in the occasional taste of gossip, Angela had not changed. She still was closest to their mother. Liliana always figured Angela's and Amara's close relationship stemmed from how similar they looked to each other. Both had olive complexions and straight black hair. They were also so close because they shared almost no personality traits. Angela could care less what others thought of her, while Amara craved their approval. Still, the two always seemed close. When Liliana thought of the bond Angela and Amara shared, she was reminded of her Confirmation. It was then that Liliana realized the two had a deep connection that she would never understand. She had asked Amara for a piece of gold belonging to her Nonna Agostina—gold is a common gift for such an important event.

"You don't want a new piece? You can pick out a piece from the jeweler in Campobasso."

"No, I would rather have something that reminds me of Nonna."

Her mother stared at her. A confused look overtook her face. She appeared unable to recognize her own flesh and blood.

"Carina, I can't do that."

"But—" Liliana's little face turned red, masking her freckles. Tears slid with ease down her face. Her mother turned away from her.

"We'll go into the city and pick out something beautiful."

Liliana shrugged her shoulders then wiped her face.

She thought of Angela's confirmation. Five years had passed since her mother rejected her request. The morning of the confirmation, Liliana stood in the corridor between her bedroom and her mother's. She listened as Amara let Angela select a piece of her grandmother's jewelry. She walked quietly toward the open door and watched as her mother latched an old gold necklace with an engraved pendant of the Virgin, a beautiful ruby in its center. Liliana tiptoed away from the bedroom and into the bathroom where she wept.

As Liliana walked with her sister away from the bakery, arm in arm, she noticed her sister wearing the necklace. The sun caught the ruby, making it look like a maraschino cherry was hanging from Angela's neck. She never mentioned the incident, worried she might seem greedy or selfish. It wasn't Angela's fault their mother hadn't let Liliana chose a piece of jewelry. Yet, her sister must have known how much she wanted a piece of their grandmother's jewelry because Liliana noticed Angela always kept the necklace hidden underneath her clothing. She also never wore it when the neckline of her tops would reveal the pendant. Seeing the necklace was another reminder of how she would never be as close to her mother as Angela. Being pregnant made Liliana more sensitive; she wanted so badly to mention it. What was the point of starting a fight over an old piece of jewelry? Liliana knew better than to be petty. She was so grateful for her sister's help, though she assumed Angela helped more because their mother insisted. Amara essentially required them to be close, reminding them that they only had each other when she and Senore Farinacci died. Their mother always nudged them to work together. After their brother died and Liliana began working at the bakery, something the family thought Guiseppe would end up doing, Angela and Liliana weren't spending as much time with each other. When the Farinacci's would leave in the morning, Angela and Amara would make their way to the dress shop and Liliana would lock arms with her father and the two would head toward the bakery. Now that Liliana was dealing with Domenico being gone and the baby on the way, the two sisters bonded; Angela understood how the women in Gildone were capable of torment. They had even found ways of making Sundays horrible.

"Liliana, remember that sweet boy, Raffaele? Whatever happened to him?" She'd been asked so many times.

"When is Domenico due back? Surely, he will be home by the time the baby arrives."

"Domenico must be thrilled you're expecting if the baby is his." It was always an older woman who would make comments like this. "I'm kidding. Though, we do know what happened with your sister." These words would come out of their mouths as if without thought of who might hear them. "It's too bad how things worked out with Angela."

Angela had a tough time, and Liliana often caught her sister looking glum. She carried herself as if she had not a care of what others said, but there were times when the rumors took a toll. On several occasions, Angela was left off of invitations and Liliana knew her sister didn't have close friends. Not that Liliana did either. Looking at Angela it seemed it was her against the town. Angela had an exotic look about her and dark eyes that carried wisdom acquired too early in life. It wasn't hard to see that when Angela smiled, notes of melancholy lingered just below the surface. Liliana wondered how many times her sister had been excluded or been the subject of snide comments and judgemental looks. In that moment, Liliana was so grateful to have her nephew Giacomo holding her one hand and Angela holding the other as they entered the church on Sundays. Giacomo was almost seven and doing well in school. Angela wanted him to go all the way to the fifth grade. After that, he'd start working the fields. He'd be good at arithmetic and reading if he went through the fifth grade. His disposition was cheery. Liliana was struck by how much he looked like her father. There were only slight hints of his father in Giacomo's face.

Angela's isolation from the other mothers in town had embittered her. Yet Angela, like her mother and sister, had the ability to fake a sincere smile and deflect the other women and their looks of oh-shame-on-her-for-bringing-that-bastard-child-into-this-church. Angela also shielded her sister from the constant questions about Domenico's return, refocusing discussions back to the women and their lives. Still, it often bothered Liliana that Angela was so much more loyal to their mother because, in the end, when their parents were gone, all they would have would be each other.

"Let's ask her now."

"Lili, it's freezing, and I haven't seen my Giacomo all day. Please, ask her Sunday."

"I'll forget." She would—the baby fed on her thoughts. "It's okay. Go home. I'll have Papa walk me home."

"And then you'll both slip?"

"Come, then." Liliana paused, then added, "You'll deny your pregnant sister?" She smiled as she broke her sister down.

"Oh, fine, but let's make it quick, some of us have—" she stopped. "I'm sorry, Lili."

"It's fine. He'll write soon. I'm sure."

"He will."

"It will be okay."

They entered the house and smelled the garlic, onions, tomatoes, and red peppers.

"Hurry, Lili," Amara was already impatient.

"Quickly what?"

"Well, today, when Senora Pollentino came for the bread, she said to ask you about how Nonna Agostina used to scare all the men in town."

Just the mention of Senora Pollentino sent blood to Amara's face and chest. That woman and her constant meddling.

"What is she talking about, Ma?" Liliana needed to know.

Amara looked up from her cooking. Her daughter's skin gave off a glow like dough lightly brushed with a rich olive oil. Her cheeks were pink from the heat of the stove and the cold winter air. Her breathing was heavy, yet delicate. Amara was unable to stop staring. She hadn't felt this way when Angela was pregnant. All the stress from Gianni's mother and all the talking caused Angela to cry often to her mother. Her pregnancy had been a stressful one. Liliana instead was a more beautiful pregnant woman. Her skin was not blotchy like her sister's had been, her crying nonexistent as far as Amara knew.

Looking at her daughter, she imagined how perfect her future grandchild would be. She thought of Agostina and the dangerous journey she'd taken to retrieve her cheating husband. Liliana was not strong enough to resist the lies Domenico might tell her. He'd keep her there, just like Raffaele had planned to do; she'd then lose another child to a different kind of war. Liliana knew Amara couldn't bear to lose another child.

"Oh, who knows what the Senora was talking about? She's too young to really remember my mother."

Liliana knew her mother was lying. She noticed her mother's hands crossed over her chest. Amara's eyes met hers, then darted towards the supper she prepared.

"Nonna was fierce. She didn't tolerate nonsense." She paused. "That was probably what she meant."

Liliana looked to Angela, knowing she had been unsuccessful. The two of them always apeared to be conspiring against her.

"Fine, I guess I'll head home."

She and Angela left their mother to finish making dinner. The sisters walked to Liliana's in silence. They climbed to the top of the hill where Liliana's house rest. They reached the front door. Angela clutched Liliana's hand in her and squeezed. The sun was nearly done with its dive behind the mountains. Liliana entered the house. and the sun's departure left behind the cold air. It was chilly inside because she turned the heat off during the day. She lit the room, and her belly led her up the stairs to the bedroom. She turned the heat on and placed her coat on the bed. She craved a hot dinner. Senora Pollentino's mention of Nonna Agostina had forced her to remember her grandmother's signature dish. As far as ingredients and preparations were concerned, there was nothing special about pizza *minestra*. It was a poor farmer's meal, and Liliana remembered hating it as a child. It was mush and lacked any flavor, but as Liliana aged, the appreciation for the dish grew.

It reminded her of Nonna Agostina, who was formidable. Agostina was the kind of woman she wished she could be. After the long day, Liliana didn't care that there was nothing gourmet about pizza minestra. There was something about it capable of returning warmth to cold fingertips and toes. It was an embrace in a forkful.

The time Nonna Agostina taught her to make Sunday red sauce always flashed back to her when she remembered her imposing grandmother. They returned from mass and began the preparations. Liliana was tasked with chopping onions and garlic. Afterward, her grandmother asked her to peel the tomatoes for sauce. As she chopped, Liliana sliced open her finger.

"Nonna!"

"What?" Nonna Agostina didn't budge. She stood over the stove, preparing the meat course.

"My finger. I cut it. It's bad."

Again, Agostina didn't move. She stared at Liliana and motioned for her to come and rinse her hand. She handed her granddaughter a dishtowel to stop the bleeding. Liliana could feel her finger throbbing. She'd cut her finger quite deeply. Her grandmother showed her how to bandage her finger, then walked her back to where she was slicing the onions. Tears from the pain and the vegetable slid down Liliana's cheek.

Agostina looked at Liliana, not blinking.

"Carina, listen. Everything keeps going even if you're bleeding. You need to learn that." She remembered her grandmother looked up and away from her, a rare gesture. Agostina was not one to be described as reflective or emotional. She did what needed to be done without complaint, only persistence. Yet, at that moment as Agostina looked up and away from Liliana's face, her granddaughter could see a lifetime of cuts, bleeding, and pain. For Agostina, life had moved forward despite being sliced into over and over again.

In the kitchen, Liliana let the hot water rinse her hands, an attempt to erase the sobbing, gossip, and frustration. She heated the oven and placed a pot of hot water to boil for the mustard leaves. She salted the water and began working on the cornbread. She had many cravings in the past months since her pregnancy began, but none as strong as this need to have Nonna Agostina's pizza minestra. The mention of her grandmother at the bakery by the Senora had placed her grandmother's memory at the front, where Domenico and Raffaele usually took precedence.

As a young girl, Liliana loved watching her grandmother in the kitchen. She remembered how she came indoors dark from the olive fields. Nonna Agostina worked alongside her husband, always needing to keep him in her sight. Though as they both grew older, Agostina seemed not to mind his spending time at the bar, leaving her alone in the house with Angela and Liliana. Her skin tanned from the olive fields and wrinkled from the sun, dried out by the summer rays. Sweat dripped carefully down her neck. Agostina washed her face with a washcloth, cleaning the sweat from her neck and arms. From there, she heated the oven and prepared to cook for the family.

Liliana envied her grandmother, who didn't need recipes. Liliana had written down every recipe she could remember, though the measurements did not make sense until she was older. She could not understand how a handful of pasta was enough for one person. She watched her grandmother prepare many dishes; Agostina would take a handful of pasta for each person and never yielded leftovers after the meal had ended. Liliana measured everything. Her grandmother, however, took the cornmeal, poured what looked like enough—and always was—into a bowl and added water until the consistency was right. She measured the salt and garlic the same way, putting as much as her mother had years before.

Liliana didn't speak when Nonna prepared the meal; she watched, out of the way. Her eyes locked onto her grandmother's wrinkled arms as she mixed the ingredients together.

"Come here, Lili."

She came, afraid of the consequence.

"The bread should look like this. Now wash your hands and help." Liliana was nine years old the first time Nonna asked for her help.

"You're the oldest, you need to watch and learn these things. That's how I learned, and that's how your mother learned. We watched. We helped."

When the minestra was cooked, Agostina removed it from the heat, draining half of the water. Liliana worked in silence, shaping the cornmeal mixture into flat circular loaves. As she shaped the dough, Nonna covered them in olive oil. The yellow circles, little suns on the baking sheet, reminding Liliana of summer as she prepared pizza minestra in the wintertime.

Nonna retrieved the loaves and took one of the disks from the pan, splitting it with Liliana. She broke the crispy crust shell with her teeth. The soft warm dough released some steam. Nonna mixed the greens with broken loaves, adding more cornmeal to the green water. Liliana's nose wrinkled in disgust. The color of the mixture was dingy, not fresh or pure like the fruit tarts and desserts at Papa's bakery.

"Now Lili, we don't serve this to the king. Pizza minestra is food so we can live."

And during the war and a long time afterward, pizza minestra sat at the table with them, a new member of the family—that and *pasta fagoli.*

The smell in Liliana's kitchen twenty-some years later reminded her of playing with Angela and seeing her brother in uniform at the table. Even though they could afford other foods, the family continued to eat pizza minestra. They never grew tired of the dish—rather the opposite. Liliana craved it often. The baby kicked. She loaded the dish which was a lumpy green and yellow slop, ugly but delicious. She ate in silence, no radio tonight. Glancing up at the door, she noticed the crucifix hanging crooked. It would need to be adjusted in the morning.

18 January 1951

My Dearest Liliana,

Happy New Year! I hope all is well in Gildone. I've been working so many long days sometimes I worry I'm not writing you enough. I've yet to hear back from you. It's strange. I thought we would correspond more frequently than we do.

I worry you've met someone. That you are no longer waiting for me. Many of the men here, even the married ones, have met new women and started new families. I think about all of you back in Gildone, and though the Venezuelan landscape is beautiful, nothing compares to our perfect Italia.

Everyone I talk to says they miss home. I miss our walks at the end of the day after many hours standing over my workbench. I'm still not making shoes, though I am making good money. I don't think it will be long before I can send you enough money to get you here so we can be together.

I don't know if you heard. I suspect you have since word does travel fast in Gildone. Andrea Napo passed away. I know you were a good friend of hers. The doctors here weren't able to explain to her husband why she died, but it seems like she may have come down with influenza. Her husband Marco is beside himself. Poor guy has four kids. He is talking about heading back to Italy. I don't blame him, to tell you the truth. This place has ample opportunity, but it's tough when your family and loved ones aren't nearby.

Lili, I hope you're still waiting for me as you said you would. If you can, please write back. Just knowing you've touched the paper I'm holding when I open a letter from you is comforting.

All my love,
Raffaele

Chapter 6

That morning in March, as Liliana faced the largest challenge of the day—dressing—snow pounded the stone roads of Gildone. It would likely melt by afternoon, but its morning arrival only made Liliana's brief commute more difficult. She began staying at Amara's because, as the months passed, Liliana struggled with her stockings and shoes. Although Liliana enjoyed the peace and quiet of her house, she was glad on mornings like these when her ankles rejected her boots that she could ask for help. Her belly grew and grew, and she worried about being alone in the night if the baby should decide to come at a most inopportune time. Still, she stayed with her parents under the condition that when Domenico arrived, she would return to her house.

She hardly slept through the night as her body prepared her for her future of nightly feedings. She knew it was time to wake when Amara started to beat the eggs with sugar and Marsala wine for a quick breakfast of *zambaglione*. Using her legs, she slid to the edge of her bed. Pulling herself up, she muttered, "That bastard, leaving me in this condition."

Seeing the snow forced her to get upset as she realized her boots were more than necessary. She wobbled down the stairs, holding the wall for support. Her big belly peeked out from her robe.

"Ma?"

"Yes," Amara said from the kitchen.

Liliana caught sight of herself in the mirror. The baby would come soon—Liliana was sure of it.

"Ma, will you help me, please. I have to start getting the bread ready for today, and Angela will be here soon."

"Eat this first. You look tired." Amara handed her the *zambaglione.*

"Did you add extra Marsala? It's freezing out." It was a colder morning than she had anticipated.

"Yes, this will keep you warm on your walk."

"Thank you."

On many cold mornings, Liliana pretended to cough. She'd talk in a whiny voice as if having not slept at all. All of this, hoping her mother would prepare the egg, sugar, and marsala treat. She loved the creamy texture of the eggs and sugar beat together, its color a subtle yellow caused by the sugar and eggs forming a whip-like treat. She remembered mornings she'd beg for it. She took a sip and felt the alcohol from the wine flush her cheeks.

#

As she and Angela waded through what would be the last snow of the season, Liliana felt on edge. The feel of her jacket was wrong, her boots were wrong. She was off. Looking out at the sleeping town, her face wrinkled in disgust, annoyed to be headed to the bakery. She wanted to be alone, more so than she already was. She wanted her body to herself, not having to rent space to this child, a child who would arrive, not having Domenico's hard-worked hands to hold on to. She wondered how long it would be before the baby would see Domenico. The women she'd heard gossiping were right; she needed to be tough. She needed to fight for Domenico. Though who was she fighting, she wondered. He still hadn't reached out to her. At this pace, would this child only know the Domenico in photos? Sure, Angela was standing next to her now, but at night, after a long day of standing and working at the bakery, it was just Liliana. She and her wriggling baby moving around kicking her as she tried to rest. At least once the child arrived, she and the baby would be together. Who knows what kind of loneliness would settle in after that? Maybe it wouldn't be so bad. She would have to care for the child night and day, which was better than simply caring for herself.

The morning was quiet, no rush of customers. Liliana planted herself in a chair that morning, finding it difficult to stand. After escorting her sister, Angela stayed with her until their father arrived to prepare the bread and biscotti. Senore Farinacci helped with the recipes Angela was unsure of. By the time he arrived that morning, the sun had melted the last of the snow, and water trickled down the streets. Liliana watched the window, waiting. She let her head lean against the wall and listened to her father and Angela prepare the dough for the sesame bread.

#

There was no warning. One moment she sat in the soft quiet of the bakery. And the next:

"Angela."

"What?"

"Angela!"

"What?"

"Angela, I need you."

"Oh, my goodness. It's time."

Frantic Angela left the dough, looked up at her father. He nodded, conceding. He would have to watch the bakery. "Okay, let's go. We'll go to Mamma's."

They passed through the town. It was quiet; the children were at school, the women prepared lunch, and the men worked in the fields. Liliana and Angela passed the center, working their way uphill towards their childhood home.

"Be strong, Lili. Be strong."

Liliana would be, too; it was genetic for her to withstand the pain this child was forcing on her. Amara had told Liliana and Angela about Nonna Agostina and her high tolerance for pain.

"You girls have to be strong like Nonna," she'd say. "The day Nonna gave birth to Zio Peppino, she worked in the olive fields. I remember it was summer; there was no school. Nonna had asked me to take care of your aunts and uncles. It was hot, and she worked until noon. It was when she stopped for lunch Zio Peppino decided it was time to join us, and so she lay down in the field giving birth to him. She didn't cry as they do now. She carried him the rest of the day and then back to the house. I prepared supper that night since Mamma looked tired." She paused, letting it sink in. "Can you girls be strong like Nonna? No crying."

As the pain surged through Lili's body, she questioned the validity of her grandmother's story. It seemed a myth now as she worked her way towards her mother's. But as they entered the house, she glanced over in time to see Nonna's photo. Her wrinkled face and tough skin would not have cried. She needed no one.

Amara opened the door as the two girls entered. Angela was calm and ready to take orders. Liliana looked afraid as tears of pain ran down her face.

"Take her upstairs. I'll be right up," Amara ordered.

In the kitchen, she boiled water and took out clean rags and towels. She carried it all upstairs.

"Angela, go get the doctor."

She left, leaving Amara and Liliana together.

"Carina, you're going to be fine."

"I don't know, Mamma," she started to say. She was scared.

"You're not the first to have a baby, and you won't be last." Amara was never one to mince words.

Liliana let herself cry briefly, then focused on her breathing.

The room was dark. Her mother had drawn the curtains and laid towels and rags on the mattress.

"Breathe, carina. You're only making it harder on yourself."

Liliana wanted to be anywhere but in her old bedroom giving birth to this fatherless baby. She imagined what it would be like to call Domenico and tell him to hurry home because the baby was coming. She looked at the curtains. The eyelet fabric let in tiny flecks of light. The sun was starting to set. In the afternoons, when the curtains were open, this room was often overwhelmed with light making it hot. The cooler spring air kept the room comfortable. Liliana stared at the curtains thinking of all the places she'd rather be than in this room.

"When was last time you felt pain?"

"Maybe five minutes ago. I'm not sure." As she answered her mother, her sides felt as if electricity was surging through them. She lurched forward. Amara pushed her back onto the bed.

"You can't do that every time you have pain. It will take longer. Trust me." She looked at Liliana, and for a brief moment, she caught a slight glimpse of empathy in her mother's eyes. Angela returned, entering the room as if by a gust of wind.

"Angela, stand next to your sister. Prop her up and hold her hand."

"The doctor will be here soon."

"That's fine. We're going to be here for a while." Liliana watched her mother take command of the room. With each breath and push, Liliana felt closer to her mother and sister. Soon, she'd be a mother just like them. Maybe one day it would be just the three of them taking on whatever the world was throwing at them. In between one round of pain and pushing and the throbbing of her belly and sides, she noticed Amara and Angela exchange a knowing glance. No, it would never be the three of them; Liliana would always be just on the edge of their inner circle, like the decorative cherry on top of a sospiri.

Liliana was pulled out of her thoughts by a pressure building up forcing her to push. She yelled out in pain and felt Angela's hand on top of hers. She took a deep breath and let the pain out with an exhale. Sweat began dripping down her back. It might be minutes or hours, but soon everything she knew about life would be different and scary, and she was afraid. Afraid to be a mother. Afraid their life in Gildone wouldn't be good enough for the two of them. Afraid to be alone. She took in a big breath and pushed her hair out of her face. She looked up, staring at the line where the wall meets the ceiling and pushed as a torrent of pain rushed her.

#

When Amara handed her the baby, she forgot the hours before seeing Francesca's tiny fingers and toes. Her perfect, little face stared back at Liliana. Liliana felt her daughter's fingers curl tight around hers. Smelling only the newborn, she took a deep breath, closed her eyes, and slept.

#

8 March 1951

My Dearest Liliana,

I woke up this morning after having a dream about you. It was a relief to see your face, though I was sad when I woke up and realized I would not see you today or tomorrow or the day after that. In the dream, you were standing along via Olivito. The farm was behind you, and your hair was down. I don't think I've ever actually seen it down, but there it was cascading down your back. The sun was kissing your face, the way I wish I could, and you were looking into the sun with your eyes closed. You looked so peaceful. Funny enough, you were wearing your apron and there was dough stuck on your fingers. When I waved at you, you waved back. I turned my head for one moment, in the dream, to avoid a car, and when I looked back at you, you were gone.

It made me wonder if you were gone. If you walk to your mailbox hoping to see an envelope with your name on it in my handwriting. Well, when you open this, I hope your heart beats a little more quickly.

Until then, I'll see you in my dreams.

With all my love,
Raffaele

Chapter 7

The days following Francesca's birth, Liliana struggled. The baby refused to feed. Both mother and daughter cried. Francesca's little face revealed pain as hunger overtook her tiny baby body.

"What do I do? I can't take the screaming, Mamma. I just can't take it."

"We need to talk to Rita."

There were three milk-mothers in Gildone, but only Rita Lacchini's milk was rumored to make the babies strong and help them to live long. Rita's milk-children were the strongest and healthiest in the town—immune to the cold, influenza, fever. She was a dramatic woman who was known for giving out recipes with missing instructions and ingredients. She was well endowed, a blessing she claimed kept her husband from traveling too far. Before they were married, her now-husband had courted her over and over again, yet she refused, unable to decide between her many pursuers. She claimed an angel whispered to her that he'd bring her happiness and beautiful children, and he did.

"Look at my sons, they are perfect." Speaking always for effect, she would add, "God gave me these." She would push her shoulders back to emphasize her breasts, looking down at them. Her face showed the weight she carried. "He must have needed me to help." And Rita had helped many children in Gildone, and her milk appeared to bond those children together. Her sons were always so close to their milk-brothers and sisters.

Amara and Rita had never been close. Amara's bitter aura isolated her from many of the women in Gildone. Rita, while a good woman, was very capable of letting loose the feline inside her. Amara was sure Rita's dislike for her was simply jealousy. Amara was the only girl Senore Farinacci courted. His mother had attempted to make her son marry Rita; both families were likely to benefit from their union. Rita was significantly younger than Amara—still, Franco was adamant about Amara. The rumor was that Rita had never been rejected, only desired by the men in Gildone, and her failure with Senore Farinacci came as a shock to the town. From the looks of it, Rita had overcome her brief wounds with her gift. It was obvious she enjoyed being needed, having power over the fate of the children and their mothers. She'd furrow her eyebrows in a delicate frown when she heard about a mother not being able to feed her newborn.

"Oh, poor, baby," she'd say and heave her breasts as if about to faint. "I'll go to her and see what I can do." And because of her love of power, Amara was sure Rita had heard of her daughter's problem. It was no secret that Liliana struggled to feed the baby. The baby cried at mass, going and coming from anywhere in town. The poor child was starving and if Liliana didn't act soon, Francesca would starve to death.

"Look," Amara began as she stood in front of Rita's door. "My daughter is desperate; she needs you." She hated to ask for help. Rita smiled as if she knew she, or at least her breasts, were needed.

"I know. I will help, but only because it isn't the child's fault whose blood she comes from." She took a breath, filling her lungs and propelling her chest forward. "It's for the child, Amara."

#

Rita sang to the child as the baby ate and ate and ate. Liliana took Francesca home, and while the baby slept, she wrote to Domenico. The paper was kept in a small drawer in the kitchen. It wasn't plain white paper but looked like paper for graphing.

There wasn't much of it. Liliana hid Domenico's cigarettes next to the paper, not wanting to see them next to the bed, reminding her that he wouldn't be arriving for dinner, yet again. She retrieved one from the box, took a match, and lit it. This time the smoke did not make her sick. As she inhaled, the smoke took over her breath. The muscles around her neck loosened. Looking at the paper, she remembered why she stood in the kitchen. She had not heard from him since his brief note, which promised money that never arrived, as well as confirmation on his not returning anytime soon. She thought about him and the Venezuelan jungle air, the heat, and the rain. Her hand pressed the pen hard into the paper; her tears wet the paper, smearing the ink.

Domenico,

You have a daughter. She is beautiful with perfect fingers and toes and a full head of black hair, which she must have gotten from you. Her name is Francesca. I'm sure she would love to meet you. Come back soon.

Your wife,
Liliana

Not caring about the smears, she sealed and mailed it in the morning.

#

4 October 1951

My Dearest Liliana,

Things are going well here. The economy here is good, and I've been able to save up. In about three months, I'll be opening up my own shoe store. I am so excited. I'll even have enough to buy a house soon. It seems that leaving Italy was the right move, though it did mean leaving you.

A few months ago, I went to Matteo Ricci's wedding. It was nice to see so many pisanos together. He and his wife are expecting, and so are my brother and his wife, Sofia. I'm going to be an uncle! I'm sad I won't be there to meet the little one, but Tonino says he and Sofia will be visiting soon. Do you ever see him? I know he's always working.

When I think of all these beautiful babies being born, I can't help but wonder, if I had stayed, would we too be having babies? Do you ever think about this? I can just see you holding a perfect baby girl. I'd want a girl. She would look like you and bake like you and only smile back when it was earned, as you do. I can just see you shaking your head. Yes, you do make people earn your smiles, my love.

As soon as the shoe shop is set up, and I'm settled, I'll send an update. It won't be much longer after that when we can finally be together.

I hope to hear from you soon.

With all my love,
Raffaele

Chapter 8

Liliana woke to Francesca's crying. Even when she wasn't wailing, Liliana could hear her little baby's voice in the night. Just when Liliana felt sleep take over, her eyes would open, thinking Francesca needed her. She was grateful to be staying with her parents as she learned to be a mother. Amara was helpful and warm. For the time being, Senore Farinacci returned to the bakery.

That morning, Francesca's little face was red from the screaming. Liliana rolled over to pick her up. Her little mouth opened like a baby bird waiting to be fed. Liliana looked at her daughter and tears fell down her face. She could feel the pressure from her milk, making her sore. She tried to feed Francesca but she wouldn't latch on, and the few times she did, nothing came out. She placed the baby's head onto her shoulder and rubbed her little back as she stood rocking from side to side hoping to quiet her. Liliana's body was tense and tired. She wanted to help her baby girl, but she couldn't and thinking of this failure made Liliana sob more deeply. She missed her bed at home and her time at the bakery. Now that most of the day was spent with the baby, she wished she could get away and bake in the solitude of the old stone building. She missed the satisfaction of a beautifully breaded loaf, and the sound of the townspeople enjoying the millefoglie. Now, all she heard was crying and screaming and unsolicited advice.

She put Francesca down in her bassinet and wiped her face. She struggled to even look at the baby. Francesca had calmed a bit, and Liliana decided it was time to bring her Rita's. She got dressed and took care to keep Francesca calm as she dressed her, though she knew Francesca could sense her uneasiness. When they were ready, she picked her up and Francesca started to wail. Liliana felt her chest fill with pain and frustration.

"Ma, I'm bringing the baby to Rita's. I'll see you later."

When she reached Rita's and placed Francesca in Rita's arms, the crying stopped. This made Liliana both relieved and angry. She was angry at herself. Angry at Rita. And angry at the baby. She wanted to be the one to calm Francesca. That was her job as her mother. Liliana felt like she was good for nothing but baking bread and stuffing cream puffs with custard.

"Carina." Rita looked so happy holding a baby." That's enough tears. You're going to get food now." Liliana refrained from rolling her eyes. She wasn't sure if Rita was trying to be mean or if she was just talking sweetly to Francesca.

Liliana reached out to touch Francesca and then reversed her hand and placed it on her waist.

"You want to see if she'll take milk from you first?" Rita was good like this. "She's clearly hungry. You might get lucky." She took a breath not giving Liliana a chance to think about it. "Come, I'll help you."

Liliana wanted to be able to feed her own baby and knew if anyone was going to be able to help her it would be Rita. She wondered if her mother would be surprised at Rita's generosity and thought it best to keep this exchange to herself.

They sat on an old sofa in the living room.

"Get comfortable," Rita ordered.

Always one to follow orders, Liliana let herself relax. She unhooked her top and got ready to take Francesca in her arms. Rita placed the baby in Liliana's arms. The baby opened her mouth and began to scream. Rita leaned forward, ignoring the high-pitched howling of the baby and placed her fingers on the side of Liliana's breasts.

"Oh, yes. There is a lot of milk here. Let's see if we can get the baby to drink it."

Rita took Francesca's head which wriggled and writhed, eager to eat, and placed it under Liliana's exposed breast. She nudged the baby up to the food source and in a delicate yet forceful motion pushed her head towards Liliana's chest.

Suddenly, Liliana felt a rush of pressure release from her chest.

"Well, she's definitely getting the milk now," Rita said smiling. She turned to leave the room. "Would you like a coffee while you feed her?"

Liliana nodded and mouthed a huge "thank you" to Rita. She worried if she moved one centimeter Francesca might lose her latch. Francesca looked up at her while she ate. For the first time in the few weeks of her daughter's life, Liliana felt like Francesca's mother.

Even though Rita nursed Francesca early on, Liliana was eventually able to feed the baby on her own thanks to Rita's help. Once Francesca was eating and Liliana was able to feed her, motherhood was a little less daunting. Francesca's sweet, little hand would gently touch her chest as she fed. Her tiny mouth would pucker when she finished eating and her head would bob back and forth as Liliana placed her on shoulder to burp her. When the baby cried, Liliana loved to pick up her up from the bassinet and calm her. Little Francesca would nestle her baby face right into Liliana's neck. She was beginning to settle into motherhood; she still worried about what to do and how she would handle Domenico's absence, but these challenges briefly faded in the moments her little Francesca looked up at her, only to return when Liliana lay awake at night alone in her bed.

She wouldn't admit it, but Liliana worried what the world would be like for a little girl. Boys, as far as everyone who volunteered the information were concerned, were easier. This was especially true when they were older. With girls, they had to stay beautiful, get married, not be too talkative, not get pregnant until they were married, and know their way around the kitchen. Boys came with a freedom that girls did not, and for this Liliana worried.

It was not helpful that Domenico had not written back even after finding out he was a father.

"Can you believe it?" Liliana was incredulous. "It's been months. He's known for *months*. And nothing. Absolutely nothing." Liliana held Francesca close to her chest, her hand resting on the baby's neck.

"He'll be back soon. I just know it." Amara knew what to say to her daughter to ease her worry, but this story had played out many times before. First the war had taken the young men in the village, and then the promise of wealth an ocean away. It was all for nothing.

"Do you think so?" Liliana wasn't convinced. Motherhood had fatigued her, and she was certain her mother was placating her. Liliana grew up seeing her mother lose Guiseppe. Even her grandfather left at some point to go to Venezuela. At least he returned. "I'm just so tired of worrying about it. I wish he'd write and let me know what is going on with his work."

"He will," Amara lulled in a whisper. "He will."

#

Francesca's first steps occurred while Liliana prepared the almond biscotti. The almonds were fresh from the Oliveta farm. The September air was far less humid, and the leaves looked as though they were getting ready to let go for the fall. The countryside was filled with burgundy, yellow, and layers of different greens as harvest time approached. Fields of sunflowers were in bloom. The windows to the bakery were open and a gentle breeze nudged the sweet aroma of Liliana's baking.

Liliana pulled the roasted almonds out of the oven.

"Pa, watch her. I don't want her to get burned."

Senore Farinacci pulled Francesca onto his lap, her little baby feet pushed up against his legs, and she stood. Her dark eyes lit up as she stared at her grandfather. Drool dripped from her dark pink lips.

He put her down when he saw the almond tray had been put down. Francesca pulled herself up using the door frame. Her hands pushed against the wall to stabilize. She was trying to get a hold of a loaf of bread that rested precariously on the edge of the counter. Her eyes fixated on the bread as she moved.

"Pa. Pa. I think she's going to walk."

Senore Farinacci stood up to see if his granddaughter would do it. Her father had asked her every day from the time she turned six months old if she was walking. He'd come home from working at the bakery, pop his head in, and ask.

"Is she walking? Shouldn't she be walking yet?"

After hearing that question for over six months, Liliana couldn't help but wonder why he was so eager for his granddaughter to be so mobile.

Her little feet took one step toward the bread and Liliana. Then she took another step. She took five steps before she petered out and her bottom hit the floor.

"Just wait until she walks," they would say at mass. "It's much harder to control them then." Liliana smiled. Maybe that wasn't such a bad thing.

Chapter 9

With a cigarette in one hand and Francesca's small five-year-old hand holding the other, Liliana worked her way towards Amara's house. She tried to bring Francesca to the bakery but preferred it when she could be alone. At first, she enjoyed watching Francesca in the bakery, but with her father officially retired, she didn't need the additional distractions, not to mention that she worried if Francesca learned to love baking she might end up just like her mother, alone and waiting in Gildone. Liliana inhaled a big gulp of smoke. As she approached her mother's house, she put out the cigarette, not wanting anyone to see her smoking. It wasn't ladylike, and her mother would disapprove.

"Hurry, Mammina needs to get to the bakery."

Francesca looked up at her mother with Domenico's eyes, her eyelids heavy. She walked with as much speed as she could. Amara answered the door before Liliana had the chance to knock.

"Hush, your father isn't feeling well." She took hold of Francesca's hand.

"Okay, I have to go. Please read her something." Raising Francesca, Liliana began to realize how smart her cousins who had gone to school in Rome were. They had smart husbands who stayed put. They weren't lonely. Liliana wanted this for her daughter and insisted that Amara read her at least one story a day. She also asked Angela to have little Giacomo, who was not so little anymore, teach his cousin to write. She looked at Francesca. "You have to be good for Nonna and Nonno. Make sure you keep Nonno company. He isn't feeling well."

"Mamma, will Nonno tell me a story today."

"I don't know. You can ask him when he wakes up."

Liliana looked forward to when Francesca would start school in a few weeks and she could get to the bakery on time. As she walked towards the bakery, she lit another cigarette. She took the long way. She was already running late. What difference would five minutes make? She wasn't going to have time to prepare the sfogliatelle for the fall festival that weekend anyway.

She held the cigarette down by her side, hoping passersby wouldn't notice. When she saw no one around, she took in more smoke, hoping it would calm her nerves. She noticed, when dressing, the wrinkles that had formed around her eyes, and the lines around her mouth were more prominent. Money was tight, but she owned her home and the bakery. Still, raising Francesca on her own was proving difficult. She was grateful Amara was around to watch her while she managed the bakery. Domenico had yet to write. For five years Liliana had checked the mail hoping that she'd see an envelope with a Venezuelan return address. She waited to see if her husband would write to his daughter. Still, she waited. Francesca knew nothing about Domenico. She only knew of him what she could glean from the one picture Liliana kept downstairs and the clothes that remained in the dresser upstairs in the bedroom. Liliana let the smoke from the cigarette drift up to her face. The smell of the smoke reminded her of Domenico, who always enjoyed a cigarette before and after dinner. His clothes smelled like cologne and cigarettes and at the first light of a cigarette, Liliana would feel the light pulling of nostalgia. The smell made her think of the late nights she and Domenico enjoyed before he left. They never said much to each other, but they did enjoy each other's company. She pictured him with a glass of brandy and a cigarette, and her holding a small espresso cut with Sambuca. It was easy to get caught up in those ineffable memories but seeing the mailman make his way down the winding cobblestone streets, she remembered how he hadn't written, how she'd been forgotten. She picked up her pace. She would need to try and get the sfogliatelle done.

She smoked one cigarette after another, thinking of Domenico the entire time.

#

The sun began to set as Liliana headed to Amara's house to pick up Francesca. Senora Pollentino sat on her balcony, overlooking the center. Most evenings Liliana was able to avoid her, but on days when her timing was off, the Senora interrogated her. The first few days she had left Francesca with Amara, Senora Pollentino noticed immediately.

"What happened? No baby today?"

"Oh no. It's tough to get anything done when she's there." The same conversation on repeat.

"Well, how is she going to learn to bake if she's not with you?" This was on everyone's mind, it seemed. Who would take over when Liliana couldn't knead the dough?

"Maybe she won't bake. Maybe she'll be a doctor or lawyer." Liliana always wished she would keep these thoughts to herself, but she couldn't help but wish more for her daughter than a lifetime of heat from an oven, trapped in a town made of rock.

"Oh, don't say that. You're the best, Liliana. She must learn from you."

"Of course." It was always at this point that she'd scurry past the senora's house.

"Any word from your husband?"

With that question, she pretended not to hear anything and kept walking. She wondered if they'd ever let her move on.

The whole town wanted to know about Domenico and Raffaele and all the other men who had disappeared. Every Sunday at mass, the women appeared kind, asking her if she needed anything.

"Lili, do you need me to watch Francesca while you're at the bakery? You've been so busy." Liliana felt somewhat accepted.

"I don't know how you do it without Domenico around. When was the last time you heard from him?" She sensed the offers and kind words were more of a means for the women to learn about her situation, only to criticize it when she wasn't looking. They had done this with each other, helped out, and watched each other's children, only to describe every bad habit and lack of mothering skills to the others. Still, as Francesca grew older and began to make friends with their children, they started to accept Liliana. She was a mother like them. Some even showed empathetic smiles when Venezuela was mentioned.

She walked through town, touching the cold stone walls, looking out onto the valley. Her feet stomped on the cobblestone in an effort not to trip. She evaded the Senora this afternoon.

#

"Go and see your father. He isn't well," Amara demanded as she opened the door.

"Did you call for the doctor?"

"He said he'd pass by in the next few days."

"Liliana worked her way up the stairs and heard Francesca talking with Senore Farinacci. Her voice was deeply concerned.

"Nonno, will you be better soon?"

"Maybe, carina."

"Did you know that I'm going to school soon?" Liliana came closer, looking through the crack to see her father nod and smile at Francesca.

"Well, the other kids are going to make fun of me because of my Papa. Is that true Nonno?"

"What? Why would they make fun of you, Bella?"

"Because he hasn't come back. The kids say Papa hates me and that's why he won't come back to Italy. Is that true?"

Liliana looked at her daughter unsure of what to say. She looked up and took a deep breath.

"Well, that's just not true. A lot of those children at school don't have their Papas either. They are in Venezuela with your daddy."

"Why is he there, Nonno?"

Senore Farinacci sat silent. Liliana could see how her father looked at Francesca's dark eyes that so resembled her father's.

"Nonno?"

He smiled at her. Francesca, though she looked so much like Domenico, resembled Liliana at that moment, who carried her quiet suffering on her face. Her eyes were heavy and a slight wrinkle formed on her brow.

"Carina, shouldn't you be getting ready for when your mother comes to get you?"

She ignored the question and observed, "Nonno, you look sad."

Liliana's chest swelled, reacting to an almost physical blow.

"No, I'm just tired, *mi amore*." He took a sad, heavy breath. "Go now, and get ready. Your mother will be here soon." Liliana stepped back, away from the door. Heading towards the stairs, she could hear Francesca gathering her things. Her little feet and hands moving towards the door, little patters on the wood floor.

When Francesca emerged from the room, she looked relieved to see her mother.

"Mamma, you look dusty." The day's work appeared on her clothes. Liliana nudged Francesca to wait for her downstairs.

"I just need to speak to Nonno."

She entered the room to see her father resting. His newspaper lay on his lap, his eyes closed. Hearing her come in, his eyes opened. His face brightened as he saw Liliana.

"You're feeling better," she said.

He nodded, sudden exhaustion preventing him from speaking. He looked at his daughter, concerned. Her father's eyes looked through her. The wrinkles around his eyes were more pronounced. His eyebrows furrowed as he brought his lips close together in concerned half-smile.

"It's fine, Papa. We're fine." They weren't. Hearing her daughter's concerns about her father was not surprising to Liliana, only heart-wrenching. She tried to explain why Domenico had left, to explain that he hadn't abandoned them, but had left in order to help them. This was what she wanted her daughter to know, but as the years had passed and she looked at her daughter, she began to forget how he had struggled to find work. She, like her daughter, was confused and upset by the loneliness. She could see her father's awareness. She was pretending—strong woman: a persona for Francesca.

"I know what will make you feel better." He smiled as she said, "Some sfogliatelle. I'll bring some for you tomorrow."

"Your sfogliatelle could heal all problems."

She had successfully changed the subject and was ready to leave. She pressed her hand into his, looked up at God, and asked Him to make her father better. As she walked back with Francesca, she wondered if it would be better if she spent more time in the bakery, but decided against it. Francesca was too energetic for the slow, relaxed pace in the bakery, and Liliana wanted to be sure her daughter wouldn't fall in love with baking as she did. She wanted her to love school so she would eventually leave this town, its gossip, and nomadic men. She thought about Angela, who was now stuck in the dress shop with Amara. Her every move, decision, and thought monitored by their mother. Liliana should have escaped with Raffaele when she had the chance. Now she'd have to wait for Domenico to call for her. She was lonely, and every so often an older man who was sweet and kind acted interested in her, but of course, she was married and couldn't do anything. Oh, the shame that would bring on their family.

She wanted better for her daughter, she wanted her to escape the stone confines of Gildone on her own and not need anyone to fall back on but herself, not trapped by any sort of dependence. Francesca would learn how strong a woman could be.

#

9 December 1951

My Dearest Liliana,

I was thinking of you as the Christmas season started. I always remember how busy you were at the bakery. There is an Italian bakery on the same street as my shoe shop. The baker is from Calabria. He has really, really good bread, but his pastries are not as good as yours. You know what they say, "The best cooks from Calabria." This might be true, but the best baker is from Gildone.

This baker has learned to make cookies from all over Italy which is really smart of him. There are so many Italians in

Valencia, but we are from all over. It's nice to go and get a taste of home.

How is everything, my love? I keep writing, but I'm getting worried. Gabriele Russo told me his mother wrote to him and said you were seeing some soldier. He said that this soldier is from a nearby village. Is that true? I know I've asked a lot of you, and I know you've had to be so patient. I just hope you're still waiting. The shoe shop is doing well. I have enough for the boat trip, but I want to make sure we can be settled and happy here. It won't be much longer.

With all my love,
Raffaele

Chapter 10

When the school day ended, Francesca walked from the school to Amara's house. Senore Farinacci was still ill, so Amara and Angela would switch off who managed the dress shop and who arrived at the house to greet Francesca. There in the basement of the house, they would sew while Francesca worked on her homework. When she finished, Amara would hear her granddaughter's feet run up the stairs so she could to read to her grandfather. She would read him anything she could find. Amara wasn't sure where Francesca's love of reading came from; it must have been Senore Farinacci; he was always reading something. Amara neglected to acknowledge that Francesca had inherited any genetic traits from Domenico's side. Since Amara determined, he had decided to neglect his own flesh and blood. It was appalling to Amara that Francesca was almost a teenager, and she had never spoken to her father, seen his penmanship on an envelope, or heard the sound of his voice.

Amara would, on occasion, sneak up to watch Francesca read to her grandfather. She saw how he listened quietly. His eyes closed, his breath deep, but the moment her voice stopped, he would begin telling her how he became a baker, and how his father had taught him. Amara had heard him tell these same stories to Liliana. On days when he had more energy, he led Francesca to the kitchen and showed her how he had taught Liliana to make bread. He challenged Francesca to make the bread as good as her mother.

"Okay, *picolina*. We put some water and work the dough. Once we do that, what's next?"

"It rests."

"That's right." He would take the bread and put a dishcloth over the top of it and place it in the oven. It would rest once more before going into the oven with a small pan at the bottom with water to make the crust of the bread brown and crunchy.

Liliana came to pick her up and oftentimes arrived to the familiar smell of crusted bread laced with oil and sprinkled with sugar, Francesca's favorite snack. Her daughter was always excited to show her mother how she had made the bread. Liliana didn't like to see her daughter so excited to bake. It would only be a matter of time before Francesca would ask her mother to take her to the bakery.

"Pa, I don't want her baking."

"I don't understand." Any happiness he kept in his face departed.

"I just don't want that kind of life for her. I want her focused on school."

"Lili, she's just a baby. She'll have her whole life for school, and she likes to bake as you used to when you were her age." He looked at Liliana, a little girl once again. "You should take her to the bakery."

"No, the only place she's going to is the library. I don't want her baking."

He sat down on the edge of a chair in the kitchen. Francesca was outside with Giacomo. The two played with marbles, fighting over a bright red and purple stone. His face was weighted with disappointment that consumed her. Still, she stood firm. Her hand reached into her pocket, aching for a cigarette. He was not easily brought down. She defeated him, and he had fallen like a platter of beautiful pastries fresh from the oven dropped to the ground, no longer salvageable.

"Lili, she has your talent. With your help, she might even be better than you."

"Always the charmer, eh, Pa." She shook her head. "Look, flattery isn't going to change my mind." She inhaled a deep breath, smelling only the bread. "I'm not going to make her feel tied down to this place like I was."

"Tied down? Who said you were tied down? You could have left whenever you wanted?"

"Do you really expect me to believe this?"

His stare met hers.

"I don't want her baking."

His shoulders sagged in defeat. Now, with this emphatic no, she'd let him down. For her whole life, he'd been her ally. His eyes looked up at hers, and he began to reach out to Liliana, only to retreat seconds later.

"Lil, baking saved you. Hell, it saved me."

She closed her eyes. He wasn't wrong.

"The bakery was always our getaway. We could escape your mother's gossiping and bickering. You really blossomed. Lili, look at how successful you are now." He sat upright and placed his hands on the table. "My goodness, Lili, people come from out of town just to try your sfogiatelle and millefoglie. Even you have to realize how incredible that is. None of that would be possible without the bakery."

"I didn't want any of this."

"Whose fault is that?"

She stepped back.

"Carina, I know it hasn't been easy these past few years, but the bakery isn't the reason why things didn't work out."

"But, I only stayed here because of the bakery."

"No, you stayed because Raffaele left."

"I—I…" She crossed her arms then moved them to her side, she kept her eyes down avoiding his. A wave of pain rushed her chest, and she looked back at Senore Farinacci. "You both said I couldn't be with him. What was I supposed to do? It would have killed Mamma if I'd married Raf—" She looked up at him, "And then Domenico came along, and here we are."

"No, you only stayed here to make us happy."

"Yeah, so? Who else could take over the bakery?" Her heartbeat quickened. "Angela can hardly powder a pastry, let alone shape one. Antonino is dead. It had to be me."

"And what will happen when you can't bake anymore?"

"I don't know. I hadn't thought about it."

"Carina, I didn't teach you to bake so you would take over the bakery. You know that, don't you?"

"I want to believe you. I really do. I just know if I hadn't been the one making the damn sfogiatelle things might be different."

"Lili, for God's sake, don't blame your decision to stay on the bakery."

"Should I have gone after him? Can you imagine? "

"You know, Lili, you wouldn't have been the first." He looked at her and nodded, "Would you really have followed Domenico to Venezuela?"

"I don't know, maybe, but I would have gone with Ra--." She could feel a tear clinging to the top of her cheek. Her eyes bore into the ground. "The bakery was why we couldn't be together."

"No, your mother and circumstance were."

"We would have been fine, Raffaele and me. He was going to call for me…"

"I know, carina. I know."

"Pa, I've been such a fool."

"Lili, how could you have known?"

"Look, I just don't want to force Francesca into a life she can never get out of." She put her head down and wrapped her arms around her chest. She could hear Francesca giggling with her cousin outside.

"Carina, it's not the baking that upsets you—it's the way it all turned out. It doesn't have to be like that for Francesca."

"No. And it won't." She didn't want to hurt her father. He had spent so many years helping her and teaching her. He had been a wonderful father. Still, she insisted. "I'm sorry, that's just how it has to be."

"But—"

She turned her back to him to leave the room.

Chapter 11

Weeks passed and Senore Farinacci still had not recovered. His argument with Liliana marked the beginning of his health's true deterioration. Liliana knew it pained him to deny Francesca access to his baking knowledge. She also knew her father didn't want her to suffer. She always appreciated this about him. Unlike her mother, her father was soft when it came to his oldest girl. He would have climbed to the top of a mountain to get a teaspoon of sugar if she required it. So, instead of teaching his granddaughter to bake, he lay in bed and let Francesca read to him. Meanwhile, Liliana hid in the bakery, consumed by her work.

The line during the dinner rush was out the door when Liliana was interrupted by Angela. The racks would soon be empty, leaving only crispy brown crumbs behind.

"You have to come quick. It's Papa."

Liliana apologized as she ushered everyone out of the bakery. She locked the door behind her, chasing after Angela.

Liliana ran up the stairs, the bedroom door was open; Francesca's ear was close to her grandfather's face. Unable to hear what he said to her daughter, she could see the confusion on her dark, little face.

"Okay, Nonno. I will," she replied. Liliana watched her daughter's dark, round eyes

process what he had just said to her. Francesca looked unsure of what to say next. He looked at Liliana and then back to Francesca. A relieved smile spread across his face. His skin which normally carried a golden hew now looked gray. Liliana rushed over to his side.

"Pa, it's going to be okay." She wasn't sure if this was true.

"Francesca, give Nonno one more hug." Liliana put a gentle hand on Francesca's back and nudged her toward Senore Farinacci. Francesca's little arms reached for her grandfather's neck. Liliana placed her hand around her father's and gave it a light squeeze. She looked at him and giving him a closed-mouth smile. She could hear her mother and sister coming up the stairs.

"Go and sit." The sound of her little feet walking in blissful ignorance brightened the room.

Amara and Angela entered the room as he closed his eyes.

Liliana looked over at her mother. Amara's shoulders began to sink and her posture, which was usually upright and confident, was curved. She had clearly aged while tending to Senore Farinacci's illness. The wrinkles around her eyes and at the bottom of her forehead were much more pronounced, more than Liliana had ever noticed before.

Liliana turned to face her mother.

"Ma, do you need anything?"

Amara placed her hands at her waist and straightened her posture. She stood just outside of the bedroom. Her eyes were on her husband. She took a quick breath with her eyes closed, letting all the air out through her nose. She shook her head.

"Are you sure?"

Her body shrunk again. She looked up at Liliana. "Yes, I'm sure.

"Do you want to be alone with him?" She asked, motioning for Angela to leave the room with her.

Without a word, she walked over to her husband and took his hand in hers. She pressed her face up against his and closed her eyes. Her other arm reached across his body. She sunk into him.

"I'll call the priest," Amara said, standing up. She turned her back and headed to the stairs. She took a distressed breath and fought the tears forming in her eyes.

Amara took each stair one at a time. She worked to keep her breathing stable. With each step, she thought about the years they shared together. She and Franco had lost a son together, watched their daughters suffer, and done everything they could to protect the Farinacci name. She lingered on the second to last step, resting her hand on the railing. She closed her eyes for a brief moment, holding on for just one more second. Once the priest arrived, arrangements would need to be made, and time would pass by like a short-lived breeze on a hot summer day.

She turned back at the stairs toward where Senore Farinacci's body rest. She thought about their last exchange. She was in the kitchen preparing supper when she'd heard Franco's voice uneasy in the bedroom.

"Raffaele..." He coughed. "Raffaele..."

She heard this and rushed up the stairs.

"Franco, what are you talking about?" He was looking out the window. The afternoon sun beamed in, and the room was warm. He turned his gaze toward her.

"Amara, I keep thinking about Raffaele."

"Why? It's been so many years since he left."

"Whatever happened to him?"

"How am I supposed to know?" Why was he asking about this now? It was strange. Had he come across one of the letters?

"You seem to know a lot of what happens around here."

She looked him square in the face. He would have disapproved of her hiding the letters from Liliana.

"I don't know." She put one hand on her waist and planted her feet into the floor. Her eyes still in line with his. She blinked.

He leaned forward.

"I wonder about him sometimes. I'm sure Lili does too."

"Hmmm." She looked away from him.

His only concern had ever been her happiness and not the well-being of the family.

She sat down at his chair in the kitchen. She let a few tears escape, wiped her eyes, and dialed the priest. When she finished making arrangements, she went back upstairs. She stood in the door looking at Liliana, who now had Francesca in her arms. She looked older; the misery of the past few years showed its wear on her face. Sadness had a cruel way of aging of the beautiful, leaving its traces deep and permanent.

Part II- FRANCESCA

Chapter 1

The smell of lentil soup hovered over the entrance of the house. Francesca was relieved of her dinner cooking duties that evening because her mother had come home early from the bakery. After years of dealing with customers, customers like Senora Pollentino, her mother often prepared hearty dinners that warmed her core. It couldn't have been too tough a day because her mother hadn't prepared *pizza minestra*. That was reserved for the hardest kinds of days, the ultimate comfort food. Unlike her mother, on rough days, Francesca preferred sweets. Liliana always brought home *biscotti brutti* or *pizzelli*, which were comforting after a long day of her classmates repeating rumors about her father's absence. It seemed the children in town knew more about her father than she did.

Francesca relished the sweets at the bakery, feeling spoiled by her mother's job. Her grandmother constantly reminded her of how spoiled she was when it came to sweets. When Amara spoke her bitter words, Francesca became nostalgic for her grandfather who had begun teaching her to bake the sweets she so craved on hard days. He had stopped teaching her only weeks before he passed.

It was going to be a cold night; Francesca could tell by the well-lit valley below Gildone. The houses looked like candles twinkling, fires burning indoors and heating the houses to prepare for the drastic temperature drop to come. She turned the doorknob and entered. The warm smell of carrots, celery, potatoes, onions, a bay leaf, and lentils seeped underneath the cracks of the doors and up the stairs to the bedrooms.

Francesca could hear the radio in the kitchen. Her mother, news-obsessed, worried about the recent student riots in Rome.

When Francesca cooked, she preferred operas that told tragic stories of unrequited love and vengeance. She often sang along, wishing the alto's voice were her own. She took the stairs, entered her bedroom, and put her school bag down. She recounted the homework she needed to complete before morning. Even though the school year was coming to end, her teachers were still assigning so much work. Starting in the fall, every morning she would ride the bus into Campobasso. There would be so many young people in the city compared to the aging Gildone. With so many men having left their young wives, there were fewer and fewer Gildonese children; Francesca's high school graduating class was the smallest in almost twenty years. Though some of the men had returned, unlike her father, there were fewer weddings to attend and fewer baptisms. Several of her friends had moved away, too. Her best friend Carla had moved to Canada only a few weeks ago. University in Campobasso meant meeting those young people hiding in the neighboring mountain towns. Amara made it very clear she wanted Francesca to stay in town and work.

"Lili, we need another girl in the dress shop, and Francesca is talented. She's been sewing since she could hold a needle and thread."

"Ma, I want her to go to school, and she wants to go to school. There is nothing for her here." She paused. "You don't think I can't use her at the bakery?"

"Well, why don't you?" Francesca cringed behind the book she was pretending to read on the balcony of her grandmother's kitchen. The door cracked just enough so she could hear. Sure, she loved baking and cooking, but she wanted to more than that.

"Ma, the bakery is what prevented me from going with Domenico and before…" Before what? Liliana's voice dropped and Francesca couldn't hear the rest.

"That's not true. You stayed to be with your family."

"Well," Liliana stopped. Francesca recognized the defeat. "It's better, she'll go to school. She says she wants to teach. I really only want her to be happy. Isn't that all a mother should want?"

Francesca was relieved to hear this. Her grandfather had insisted she do everything and anything to make herself happy— to make her own luck, and she believed going to school would help her do this. Why was her grandmother always trying to interfere? Her mother was right to make her pursue an education. Francesca's schooling was her pass out of Gildone. Her mother never allowed her to help at the bakery even though Francesca was pretty good at baking. Before her grandfather died, she remembered backing bread with him. Right before he died he had stopped showing her. She figured it was because he had gotten too sick. While her mother was at the bakery, she and her grandfather would read. Her mother rarely mentioned Nonno Franco and how he taught her to bake. A few times, Francesca would come home from school and catch her mother baking one his favorite loaves of bread. Liliana could practically braid the dough with her eyes closed. She would see her mother dabbing her eyes with the clean part of her hands. Just like reading was Francesca's refuge, baking was her mother's. Though mother loved to bake, and worked hard to be the best baker in Gildone, it was clear she disliked some of the customers.

On Sundays, she watched her mother avoid the other women and the other mothers who stood next to their husbands, trophies. They had managed to hold on to their husbands, not lose their title: Wife. Her mother was still married legally, but Francesca was sure her parents hadn't spoken to each other in over a decade. Francesca often thought about what her father looked like and what his voice would sound like saying her name. She never asked Liliana, thinking it would probably hurt her.

When she was about six-years-old, Francesca found an old photograph of her father. It wasn't the same picture as the one in a small frame in the living room, it was a photo from her mother and father's wedding. Her mother's hair was pulled up, and she wore a small beaded cap that covered part of her hair. A small veil covered the top half of her face. Her mother looked away from the camera. To her left, her father stood. His arm wrapped around her mother's waist. He was looking at the camera with a big grin. Seeing her father's dimples made her appreciate hers. He wore a dark grey suit with a flower pinned to the lapel of his jacket. His hair is dark and shiny. Her father's eyes are round and dark. His skin a dark olive color like hers. His beard was starting to come in and a slight shadow appeared along his pronounced jawline. Francesca kept the photo in a shoebox underneath her bed with some marbles, a Barbie doll, and her play jewelry. At night, after her mother had gone to sleep, she would take the photo out and stare at it. She would whisper to her parents in the photo, telling them about her day and who she played with it at school. She would tell him about her favorite book or how Nonna Amara had taught her a different stitch for sewing.

Her mother was abandoned by her father and now lived a solemn life, and though she was still quite beautiful and desirable. Francesca had heard a few men trying to be a companion to her mother, yet her mother refused.

"Ma, he's nice. He likes you."

"Francesca, I'm married. To your father. Can you imagine how it would look if I was with someone else?" Her father had really damaged her mother.

She hated how her father was a mystery to her. She had only seen two photos of him. One of those photos was in a small wood frame in the living room. He was young and handsome in a soldier's uniform, before the war. He had sharp masculine features, his jawline evident even from the head-on angle of the photo. His eyes were large and dark with eyelashes most women would do anything for. His complexion was olive like hers, and his years of outdoor labor were clear on his dark neck.

Francesca wanted to forget she had a father. How much easier it all would be if she would just forget he even existed? But when she looked into the mirror applying eyeshadow and mascara or brushed her thick dark wavy hair, she had the opposite resemblance of her mother. From the color of their hair to the shape of their eyes, they looked nothing alike.

"It's incredible," Angela would say. "The only indication that she is your mother is the way you both freckle in the sun around your nose, and of course, your hands. My goodness, your hands are identical."

As a young girl, Francesca hated that she had her mother's hands. Liliana's hands were coarse and used. They were working hands. Francesca took good care of her hands, trying to avoid any similarities, but as she grew older, she realized how skilled her mother's hands were as they formed the sfogliatelle, or braided the bread, or filled the millefoglie. Liliana was brilliant with her hands.

"But, do I look a lot like my Dad?"

Angela looked at her, brushed her hands across Francesca's hair, moving strands away from her face. "Well, you don't really look like your mom. That is for sure."

Her resemblance to her father worried her as she grew older. She was certain that looking like him was correlated to acting like him, too. She wondered if her mother ever looked at her and saw her father. Was she a continued reminder of the way things turned out for her mother? A woman abandoned in her prime?

She could see some of herself in him. His face was serious, like hers. She and her father shared the same dark, thick, wavy hair. It was evident from the photo why her mother had married him; he looked like a protector. And though she wanted to eventually marry, she would live differently from her mother, who married old (at least that was what her grandmother said) and didn't think of herself, only others. Francesca watched her mother, desperate to please Amara, Senore Farinacci, even Zia Angela. And they were never pleased, always pushing her mother for more. Liliana was stretched so thin like dough so delicate that she tore.

Francesca stood in her bedroom, inhaling the lentil soup. She changed into some old clothes and headed down to the kitchen to help her mother. Francesca could tell by the way her mother reached for her cigarettes that she was ready for bed. Liliana's aging hands shook; she looked up at her daughter who watched her get ready to smoke and put her finger over Francesca's mouth Her mother took up smoking soon after her father left, and though she tried to keep it secret, everyone knew. And no one cared, but her mother was her mother, so she worried about what others thought.

"Go, take it outside. I'll finish up here." She pushed her mother out the door and heard the match ignite. Taking some of the day-old bread her mother had brought home from the bakery, she sprinkled it with olive oil. Her mother insisted that day-old bread was just as good when put back in the oven. Francesca respectfully disagreed, arguing that the crust was always too tough and the inside too dry. As the temperature dropped with the sun, Francesca let the heat from the oven warm her.

When her mother finished her cigarette, she returned to set the table. She covered half the table with the flowered brown, orange, and dark lime tablecloth. She served herself and Francesca the soup, and the two sat in silence, eating dinner, the way they had for Francesca's entire existence. Like a memorized recipe, it was easy to follow, familiar, and somewhat comforting.

10 March 1952

My Dearest Liliana,

How are you, my love? I have yet to hear from you. I keep wondering if you and your family moved. So many of our pisanos left for Canada. I would think I would have heard something by now. I will try and find out so that I can make sure I'm sending these letters to the right address.

I wanted to send you an update on the shop. It's really coming along. Business is steady. In the next few months, I'll be hiring an apprentice, and then buying a house. I almost can't believe it. It seems like it's taken so long to get here.

A few months ago, Emmanuelle Carfalo moved back to Italy. Do you remember him? He was in my class. We are the same age. He did well here and made quite a bit of money and was able to go back. The thought of working the fields like my brother is not something I want to do. You understand, Lili. Don't you?

I've watched you bake. I used to love watching you braid the dough for loaves. You always made sure to be so delicate and careful. It brings you so much joy. This is how I feel when I'm making shoes. I love working the leather and finishing each shoe. It's an art form, just like baking. The fields are lovely and the countryside is beautiful, but it's back-breaking work. I don't want to do that forever.

I hope to hear from you soon.

With all my love,
Raffaele

Chapter 2

Returning to Gildone every evening on the bus reminded Francesca that she had, in fact, left. The year before she started university, she noticed that living in Gildone was a trap, and living there permanently after she graduated would be a very last resort. She didn't understand why her mother refused to move the bakery. She could be successful anywhere. She really was the best baker south of Rome, possibly in all of Italy. She wished her mother would move the bakery to Campobasso. Francesca would bring it up to her mother, again.

She entered the quiet house and unloaded her work onto the kitchen table. When her mother entered the house, she looked up from her work and smiled. Her mother returned the smile.

"How was the bakery?"

"The same as always. It gets so busy in the afternoons."

Francesca delighted in the opportunity to bring up her idea.

"Ma, you know people come up here just to get your pastries. If you moved the bakery to Campobasso, you'd do so well, and I would be close to school and wouldn't have to ride the bus every day."

"No, I'm not leaving. I'm here now. This is fine."

"Is it fine?"

Her mother was always so quick to shut down her ideas.

"I'm too old to do these kinds of things."

"Why? What's so great about this town? What is keeping you here?"

"Oh, Francesca. Not this again."

Francesca left it at that, going up to her room. She didn't understand her mother's attachment to this place. Her father wasn't here. Her grandmother had Zia Angela to take care of her. Why couldn't they start over?

#

Graduation was only a semester away; Francesca was eager to spend her days in Campobasso. She worried about her mother, who would be left spending more time alone in Gildone, a place that hadn't evolved with the rest of Italy. As her mother aged, Francesca noticed how similar she had become to Amara. She spent much more time at church, going to mass daily before starting her day at the baker and even praying the Rosary while she waited for pastries to finish baking. Although the religion didn't bother Francesca—she felt it gave her mother an outlet like the baking—she worried how her mother would cope with being alone. She would eventually have to leave the Molise region when she graduated; jobs for the educated were sparse there. Her mother would be upset, but she'd survive. Liliana was like the stone Gildone had been erected from strong, wind-beaten, and, in some places, cracking.

Her mother seemed to always have a cigarette in her hand. After a long day at the bakery, her mother would sit in the privacy of their patio with an espresso and a cigarette. Liliana always liked the quiet, and after a day of customers, Francesca knew that her post-work coffee and cigarette were nearly as sacred as her time spent praying. The smoke from the cigarette would travel around the patio and ebb around Liliana's face.

Returning from school one evening, Francesca walked past her mother and the swirl of smoke surrounding her. Her mother sat with her legs crossed. Her left hand touching the small espresso cup, the right holding her cigarette. She held the cigarette between her index and middle finger, barely touching it. Her chin rested in the palm of her hand. The cigarette gave off a bright orange glow and ash collected at the end of the cigarette. Liliana sat with eyes skyward, the white smoke dancing near her face. If Liliana were to be painted, it would be this moment that Francesca would want to capture. She looked tired, yet at peace.

Francesca recalled a photo of her mother before she'd been married; her once smooth and fair skin now showed wrinkles like leather that had dried up in the sun. Her demeanor, too, had changed. Francesca remembered her mother always working to mask the pain her father had inflicted, her mind only far off somewhere when she baked. As time passed, Francesca noticed her eyes had lost their fire, as if Liliana were overworked dough with all the air kneaded out of it. And while the dullness eased the worries of how the town perceived her, she still hid her smoking from them. She had also begun to pull herself away from the other women in town, even more so than when Francesca was a child. She couldn't really remember her mother being especially close to any of other women in Gildone, aside from Zia Angela and Nonna Amara. And as she pulled away from the town, she regressed, becoming more and more old-fashioned.

Francesca retrieved the mail, began supper, and waited for her mother to finish her evening smoke. Since she had begun school, her mother left her at the bus stop, kissed her on the forehead, and went to work. On mornings when early preparation needed to be done at the bakery, Liliana left Francesca *zombagolie* in the refrigerator, knowing how much her daughter loved the sweetness from the sugar and Marsala wine.

Usually, there was no mail for Francesca to retrieve, and on the few occasions, there was, it usually came from America or Canada, reminding both Liliana and Francesca of those who had gotten away; those who had taken advantage while they could. They sent money and photographs to the less fortunate. Amara's brother, Nicolino, who worked in New Jersey as a tailor, sent Amara, Angela, and Liliana money regularly. It was always in a first-class envelope with red, white, and blue stripes, and always on the top right-hand corner were two beautiful American stamps. The money was wrapped in newspaper, cloth, or butcher paper to disguise its contents.

Francesca took the envelope from the mailbox, which had been reinforced by nails years before. She noticed the wear on the edges; it had taken its time arriving. The return address was foreign, written in a hand unrecognizable to Francesca. The city: Valencia. Valencia, Venezuela.

It was addressed to her mother. Her maiden name was written with deliberation: FARINACCI; the hard capital letters shouted at Francesca. She wanted desperately to open it but didn't. Her mother would probably be upset enough by what was inside. She set it down at the center of the kitchen table. In the kitchen, she prepared her favorite snack of olive oil, bread, and sugar. She sat at the table, her books next to her on the floor. She stared at the envelope.

It had to be from him.

Chapter 3

Liliana returned to the smell of onions, garlic, and pancetta sautéing. Francesca always enjoyed the Roman dish and made it whenever the ingredients were available. She opened the door and the aroma of the carbonara hit her. She inhaled the smell, relieved that she didn't have to cook and glad that she raised her daughter well, despite not having Domenico around to reinforce rules as a father should. She entered the kitchen to find the table not set; instead, it was covered in Francesca's schoolwork. There were books and papers everywhere. She would begin working in less than a year, and Liliana could see her daughter's enthusiasm for teaching and school continue to grow. She not only loved the material, but it was obvious what Francesca enjoyed most about school was that it wasn't in Gildone.

Liliana cleared the table, placing Francesca's books on a chair. The papers she stacked in a neat pile. As she made room for the tablecloth and dishes she saw it there, blue, red, and striped. It had traveled from far. She could see the dark letters of her maiden name carved into the delicate envelope paper. She recognized the handwriting immediately. She reached for it, leaning against the table for support.

Francesca watched her mother while draining the pasta. She returned the pasta to the pot and added olive oil to prevent the fettuccini from sticking. She pushed a chair towards her mother who stood as if the floor was disappearing from beneath her.

"Ma, what is it?" She knew already but wanted to be sure her mother did too.

"I think it's from your father." She looked at it, not wanting to open it, sure it contained something toxic.

"Well, aren't you going to open it?"

"What for? He decides he can write almost 20 years after you're born. That man…"

He had not responded to the news of Francesca's birth. And although his family did live in a neighboring village, Liliana never recovered from their lack of affections for Francesca. She was their grandchild, after all. He and his family ignored the fact that Francesca existed, even though their genes inhabited her veins. They never spoke ill of Liliana. They simply stayed away. Liliana convinced herself they were ashamed of Domenico's behavior, and this was why they acted that way.

Liliana felt pity for her daughter who knew nothing of Domenico's family. Because his family didn't live in Gildone, Francesca never saw them or learned the traditions her father had grown up with. She imagined Francesca felt as if a piece of her was missing, some unknown ingredient that pulled it all together. Francesca's strong resemblance to Domenico made his family's neglect all the more difficult to digest. She looked hard at the envelope, deciding she would be the better person and open it, not ignore him as he had ignored her.

She took a knife from a kitchen drawer and unsealed the envelope. A thick packet of papers emerged, pushing their way out.

"What's all this?" she said.

"Well, read it, Ma. You're killing me." Francesca tried to lighten the mood, though, from the dense mass of papers, she could see there was nothing light about it. She returned to the pasta, adding the pancetta, as well as the egg and cheese mixture to the pot. Francesca watched her mother's face.

Liliana put the papers down and reached for the cigarettes. She took a match and lit one, taking in a big inhale. The smoke circled her face. As far as she could remember, her mother's face was always laced with sorrow. Her big, dark eyes appeared to be far from Gildone. Francesca had seen photos of her mother as a young girl. Liliana's face had changed. The distant look was not genetic but had taken years for it to become permanent. Her mother was a beautiful woman, but the years of hardships, neglect, and pain forced her beauty to fade. Francesca hoped she wouldn't end up like her mother and was determined not to. Her mother's effort at avoiding preventing this had been fruitful. She watched as Liliana's eyes scanned the papers, each page seemed to add another wrinkle to her face.

She put the pages down, still not finished. She reached for another cigarette and lit it, inhaling deep.

"What does it say?"

Liliana looked up at her daughter. She didn't want this kind of life for her. Francesca wouldn't live like this. Davide, her boyfriend, was a good boy. She could see his sincerity towards Francesca when he sat across her from at the Farinacci Sunday lunches. It was genuine, not hungry like Domenico. Davide's eyes, brown eyes, reminded her of Raffaele, who looked almost inebriated when he was around Liliana. Raffaele seemed overwhelmed with emotion for Liliana. Though Raffaele, too, had left and faded without a single word to her.

She was sure when she married Domenico that he felt the same way for her and struggled to understand what had kept him away for so long. Those first few months of marriage were delightful. Liliana had overcome her fears of being with a man and enjoyed lying in bed the mornings before mass. She also enjoyed cooking for him and bringing him treats from the bakery. So why had he not returned? Domenico had promised; so had Raffaele and many other men who stayed behind, enveloped by Venezuela.

Among the legal documents that she held in her hand was a letter in Domenico's scribble.

Liliana,

I'm writing to ask you to sign these papers so we can be divorced. Let us stop pretending that I'm going to return to Italy. I think about the two of you often, and I'm sure you've done well without me. You were always a strong woman.

I'm married to another woman, who doesn't know I was married in Italy or about Francesca. We have four children. I'm happy here. I need this divorce so that our marriage can be official here in Valencia. I know leaving you behind was wrong, but I was young and afraid then. I didn't know things would turn out this way. Please, sign the papers so we can both move on with our lives.

Domenico

She hated him.

What a fool she'd had been, baking and waiting for him to return. Here he was, asking her for a divorce so he too could move on with his life. She had been trapped for years. Alone and unable to move on.

Angela had suggested Liliana get her marriage annulled when Domenico hadn't returned after five years. For all she knew, Angela suggested, Domenico could be dead. Not to mention, some of the older, single men in Gildone appeared to be genuinely interested in her. Liliana knew the church wouldn't allow an annulment—she'd been married and gone into the marriage willingly. Francesca was proof. She was also convinced that an annulment wouldn't have mattered when it came to being remarried. She had been relatively young when Francesca was born. Her mother disagreed with all it all. Amara reminder her that Liliana came attached with scandal. Now Domenico had the four children he desired. How could he have done that to

Francesca? She had never seen his face, had no idea what parts of hers resembled his.

Bastard.

"He wants me to divorce him." She looked back at the letter and handed the legal documents to Francesca. She tucked the letter from Domenico into her apron, not wanting Francesca to learn about her half-siblings. It seemed wrong to tell Francesca what a horrible man she came from, he had helped make her. Liliana didn't want Francesca to think that by speaking poorly of her father she was speaking poorly of her daughter. She could see Francesca growing into a beautiful woman. Unlike herself, Francesca was going to be happy. Knowing her father abandoned them for another family would destroy any ignorant bliss she lived with. She would tell Francesca later how she really felt about her father. Telling her now might ruin her make it hard for her to trust Davide, though, he was a good man who would love and take care of Francesca, the way Raffaele would have if Liliana had been brave enough to go away with him.

It was enough telling Francesca about his wanting a divorce. Her good little Catholic heart would not take it well. She tried and tried to keep her daughter happy, and she did this by trying to stay happy herself. Liliana scanned the kitchen. Francesca leaned against the counter. Her long hair, dark and thick like her father's, reached the middle of her back.

Francesca watched her mother scan the papers. Liliana's expression did not look familiar to Francesca, who had seen her mother concentrate at the bakery. For once, Francesca saw her mother reacting to the present and not the past. Francesca wanted to shake her mother to remind her that what happened, happened. There was nothing she could do to take it back.

Francesca thought about all the times she stopped into the bakery. She'd peeked in the back as her mother worked. Liliana worked in bliss, her daughter watching. Although Liliana was working, it didn't seem that way to Francesca. Her hands understood the ingredients, and they did as she commanded. The thin dough of the sfogliatelle never stuck too closely. Francesca watched as her mother shaped the dough, then, in a most gentle hold of the shell-shaped pastry, filled it with the custard, trapping it inside. Francesca loved watching her mother sprinkle each pastry with sugar. She stood silent at the backdoor, her mother not noticing. Liliana's hands, arms, fingers, and eyes focused, in conversation with the bread dough. The section she braided floated one over the other. Liliana would take just a handful of sesame seeds, always the perfect amount to cover the loaf.

Francesca wondered what her hands would say to the dough. As a child, she imagined her mother's hands serenading the sfogliatelle. How else could they turn out so perfectly? Although her teacher, even Francesca's grandfather's overworked hands were unable to shape them as precisely as Liliana.

"It's her fingers. You have them too. I taught her, now I'll teach you." He'd roll the dough thin-thin-thin. Each time she tried to work the dough, it tore.

"Your Mamma used to tear the dough, too. Be careful, if the dough tears, the filling escapes. Then the best part goes free."

Francesca struggled with the process. Even after her little hands grew, she was unable to shape the dough into the proper shell shape. She practiced on her own, but the sfogliatelle were either too small or the filling found the cracks, breaking free of the confining thin shell-shaped wall.

Francesca grew frustrated with baking and found more pleasure in cooking, relieved to press the eggplants and sauté. At the bakery, her mother could hide, escape with the ingredients, molding different shapes; using the same recipes could sometimes yield different outcomes. Francesca was sure this was comforting for her mother. When Liliana worked, Francesca could see her mother's mouth pulled back in a slight smile, just noticeable to Francesca who was familiar instead with her mother's quiet pain.

Her mother was still holding the letter. Francesca looked at her mother whose day had taken a turn after baking in bliss. Her father managed to always find new ways to hurt them. Francesca's stomach sank as filled with raw dough. Her face grew hot. She placed her face in her hands, trying to hide the tears from her mother. Liliana walked over to Francesca and wrapped her arms tightly around her daughter as if trying to heal them both with the embrace.

She returned Liliana's hug. She felt her mother needed her as much as she needed her mother. They were a team who fought to survive and be happy. Francesca was grateful her mother hadn't forced the baking on her the way Nonno Farinacci and Nonna Amara had forced it on Liliana. Although Liliana loved it, she was trapped in a bakery located in Gildone, barricaded by ancient stone walls and nestled in the mountains.

When asked about Domenico, she smiled, nodded, and responded with, "No, I haven't heard from him, but what are you going to do?" She never showed her anger, regret, or pain with anyone. Her mother learned to put on a show for the town. When the townspeople saw her at the bakery, they assumed she had moved on from the heartbreak of Domenico's leaving and Raffaele's abandonment. She was surviving, going to mass, and raising a daughter who avoided trouble. Her mother, Amara, hadn't been unable to do this. But Francesca knew she needed to live beyond the mountains that nestled Gildone. Francesca would break free.

Francesca's glossy eyes penetrated the floor; she swallowed the air caught in her throat and artificially smiled. No one divorced. It was unheard of. Sure, it didn't look good, but maybe this was her father finally doing the right thing. If they divorced, her mother could finally move on. Her father leaving had always defined her. All these years later, folks in town still asked her about him.

"Ma, you should sign it."

Liliana looked up.

"What?"

"You should sign it. He's right. You can finally move on." Her mother pursed her lips and wrinkled her brow. She looked up at Francesca and softened her face.

"I don't think I can do that." Liliana sat down. The legal papers were strewn across the table, another mess to clean up.

"Ma, I know this hurts, but wouldn't it be best to just end this story here? Right now?"

Her mother's eyes stared hard at the papers on the kitchen table. Francesca didn't know much about her father. She only knew of the one photo in the den. Her mother never talked about him, neither did her grandparents. As a child, she wanted to meet her papa. She wanted to see if he too had beauty marks covering his arms as she did. Was his hair dark and wavy like hers? Did he love sweets and fresh bread?

She imagined him knocking on the door, and entering with a simple "*permesso.*" She would stand in the kitchen, her back turned to him, and she would feel his fatherly presence, then turn and embrace him. Of course, he deserved a slap for crushing her mother's heart with one squeeze. She was half of his flesh, and she wondered if he ever thought of her. Each night as a young girl, after many lengthy prayers, she'd whisper, "God, please. I want to see my Papa," just loud enough to let the night hear it too.

"Fine, we won't talk about him, but I do need to know, are you going to divorce him?"

Liliana noticed Francesca's hands shaking. She stood up from the table and took her hands. She pulled her daughter in close for another a much-needed embrace.

"No. I'm not going to. He doesn't deserve to be free."

#

8 August 1952

My Dearest Liliana,

Forgive my delay in writing to you. The shoe shop is quite busy, and things in Valencia are changing so quickly. People from Italy arrive here often. It almost feels like home, though nothing compares to beautiful Italia.

When I left two years ago, I never thought I would be able to stay away for so long, but you know how it is when you work, the time passes and before long, everything has changed. A few weeks ago, Nicolino Di Mentra, you remember his sister, the one who married the pharmacist, tried to introduce me to a "nice girl." Everyone around here is always so worried that I haven't married. So many of the men arrived here and married even before they had jobs. I told Nicolino I already had a "nice girl." He laughed. I don't think he thought I was serious.

Of course, I am not one to joke about you. Everything I have done has been so I can be with you. You know I spend a lot of my time daydreaming, probably too much time, but when I do I can't picture myself with anyone but you, Liliana. Even in my dreams, there is only you.

Perhaps when I close my eyes tonight, I'll see you. Until then, Lili.

With all my love,
Raffaele

Chapter 4

Each morning, as Francesca waited to get onto the bus for Campobasso, she could smell her mother at work. The warm nutty scent of baking bread took over Gildone, especially during wintertime. The winds that pushed through the mountains would carry the smell under the cracks of doors and windows. She waited for the bus, inhaling the smell while studying on the small bench that rested against a stone wall. The trees were bare and dripped the winter rain onto Francesca's umbrella. The bus arrived, spraying cold water onto the sidewalk. She inhaled one last time, deciding *pasta fagiole* would be appropriate for dinner with a side of day-old bread from the bakery.

She stepped on the bus, thinking of the old-world food. The beans and pasta were stored in *la cantina*, with the rest of the winter hoard. This was where all the villagers kept their foods; in small cantinas located in the basements of their homes. Francesca would hide in *la cantina* as a young girl, but only in the summertime to escape the heat. She loved to look around and admire the food, the packaging, and imagine the possibilities. The bus weaved through the winding mountain roads, carrying a full load of lucky passengers away from the antique villages where time moved too slowly. Each day, the lucky busloads of citizens escaped the timeless stone walls for work or school. When the bus finally stopped near the university, Francesca was reminded of the actual time in history she lived in. In Campobasso, the women wore eccentric pieces of jewelry to pull together fashions established in Rome, Milan, and Paris. They wore wild colors around their eyes; confidence radiated through their funky printed tops and tight pants. Francesca attempted to dress less conservatively, though she hated the reactions of her mother and Amara who constantly questioned her updating wardrobe. Zia

Angela, however, loved seeing some of the wild outfits that were a refreshing contrast to the simple tees and skirts most of the women in the small villages wore.

The city was filled with stands for food and small bakeries, and cafés were full of young people, eating and talking and likely discussing the political unrest up north. Almost daily, another terrorist bombed an important Roman political office in the name of Fascism. The young students around Italy rebelled against their parents' generation who still had not recovered from World War II. In Gildone, the bakery filled only with the elders a couple of hours before any meal was served. It was only on Sundays that Francesca was reminded there were young people in her village. Not all the youth attended mass, only the few that refused to disappoint their religious grandmothers and mothers. Francesca enjoyed mass; it served to reset her week and keep her centered. Catholicism gave her something to have faith in. She was not like the rest of the people her age that attended mass. She did not gather in the small shadowed corner near the church's entrance. She stood and knelt, her hands together with fingers pointed up at God, praying to survive university and ultimately escape the mountain's clutches.

Francesca entered campus, passing the student protests complaining about Italy's current political state. She arrived at class early and sat down next to the door. Rushing flustered Francesca. She had evolved to be so much like her mother and grandmother, who arrived early for every occasion, especially mass. As a child, her mother explained, "Praying before everyone arrives makes it easier for God to hear you. Now, be quiet and listen." Liliana would then kneel and pray until mass began.

"I'm sure you've all heard what happened in Bologna last month." Professor Nucci entered the room in mid-sentence. He swung his briefcase onto the small desk at the front of the room.

The students began to take their seats. A few stood next to their friends finishing up their conversations.

"We've got to do something about these Fascists." He slammed his hands on the podium. "Yes!" A student echoed in the. The class hadn't started yet, but it was clear Professor

Nucci was ready to get into a political debate. It was the only the second week of class and the bombing had happened a month ago, but the country was still on edge. The news was filled with stories of arrests and conspiracy theories.

Francesca heard a vocal grumbling from a nearby student. Professor Nucci looked up from his podium.

"Okay, let's start. Who has their outlines for their teaching unit complete?" Francesca took her seat near the front and placed her bag in the chair behind it, saving it for Davide, who was perpetually late and usually arrived as their professor took attendance or began a quiz. They established this seat-saving system after they became a couple. Francesca questioned if she would have ever noticed Davide had he been a punctual person. And semester after semester she sat closer to the door, often leaving a seat open for him so he could slip in and out of class, nearly unnoticed.

Davide always found a seat closest to her in all the classes they shared, yet they hardly spoke. And on top of his consistent tardiness, Francesca noted that Davide carried himself differently from the Molise natives. He wore his hair longer than most and wore the latest trends. He had phased out his 1970's elephant pants for hip, white-pleated pants. Everything about him was particular, right down to his pinky ring. His chaotic yet cool appearance appealed to her. It started with Francesca catching him looking at her during class. At first, she wasn't sure what to make of it. In Gildone, the boys her age weren't subtle in their advances. She would look back at him and smile. This went on for two semesters before Davide gathered the strength to ask her on a date. Though sometimes Francesca wondered if his flirtations had simply broken her down. She debated refusing him since he had taken so long to ask her, but his sweet eyes and cool demeanor had charmed her.

"Carina," she turned to look at him.

"Sì."

"I was thinking we could explore Campobasso this weekend. Come and have *un piccolo café.*"

She turned away from him, trying to cover up her flushed face, relieved that unlike her mother whose fair skin always showed the rush of blood to her far, her olive complexion protected her.

Why not? What was the harm in a little coffee? She tried to attempt an indifferent tone, but a cheery, high-pitched "Yes" escaped her lips.

After exchanging phone numbers and deciding on a meeting place, they walked away from each other. Francesca was glad he had initiated the date; she was much better at being chased than at chasing.

Learning he was from Rome and not from nearby explained his seeming so alien. Francesca liked this about him. As their graduating year approached, Francesca wondered if Davide would return to Rome. He stayed with his grandmother in Ferrazzano, a town that rested even higher up in the mountains than Gildone. Francesca was certain he could help her escape the mountains. Liliana worried the two would separate after graduation. They had been dating for a long while, and there was little talk of marriage.

"I don't understand, you've been dating for two years. What does he want from you?" Amara pushed Francesca for answers.

"What does it matter, I know he loves me. I don't want to pressure him."

"Sometimes they need pressure." Amara's face tensed. She scrubbed a pan with a scowl on her face. Her grandmother was always worried about everything.

"Is he going back to Rome?" Liliana asked.

"I don't know. We haven't really talked about it."

"Mah, can you believe this?" Amara raised her voice. She slammed her hands into the water and sprayed soap all over the counter. "Tell me, then, what do you two talk about?"

"Ma, lower your voice. The boys are only a room away," Angela warned.

"And if he goes back," Amara continued softly now, "are you going to go with him, and leave your mother?"

Francesca's eyes met Zia Angela's, who tried to show some empathy. The closer graduation approached, the more aggressive Amara became about the family being separated. Liliana, though excited for Francesca, knew she would struggle with more loneliness when her daughter finally left Gildone.

"All right, leave her alone," Angela broke the tension. "She's young. Let her live her life."

"Angela's right, Ma. Enough," Liliana chimed, relieved she didn't have to be the first one to say it.

Defeated, Amara finished cleaning and prepared the espresso.

Liliana understood her daughter's need to go with Davide, should the opportunity present itself. She wanted Francesca to be happy. She wouldn't guilt her into staying in the small town which offered nothing but loneliness and isolation. She was relieved to think Francesca wanted to leave for bigger and better places.

Amara worried what Francesca's departure from the family would do to Liliana.

"She's off gallivanting with that boy in the city. Lili, it worries me."

"What for? She likes him, and so do I. He reminds me so much of Raffaele. You've seen the way he looks at her." Her throat was dry and she found it hard to swallow. How many times had Raffaele looked at her the way Davide looked at Francesca?

"And what good he did for you? Eh?"

Amara hated when Liliana brought him up. His intercepted letters hid in a shoebox, in a kitchen drawer. Amara had stopped reading them, only adding new ones to the collection as she received them. She took a deep red satin ribbon and bound them together. It would kill Liliana to see them, to know he had called for her as he promised. She'd thought of burning them, but wasn't able to bring herself to do it. Everyday Amara watched as her daughter grew bitter and hard, like bread left out too long. She could see Liliana was jealous of how full her sister's life was. Angela now had three more children and a husband who would never abandon her. Gianni had been given the chance to leave her when she told him about Giacomo. Instead, he fought with his family to be with her.

Gianni and Angela arrived at Amara's house, always loud and laughing or fighting. Angela's life had flavor. Liliana always envied her sister; Angela did as she pleased. At some point, Liliana noticed, the women in town had stopped caring and moved on to the other gossip; rumors like how the other bakery was going to close and there would be a takeover of the butcher by some other family. Had people heard that so and so was working and trying to raise her children? Cluck, cluck, cluck. None of it was about Angela, who had a beautiful family. Instead, Liliana was deserted. No letters from Raffaele arrived. He had likely settled down and forgotten his promise to wait for her. Just like Domenico, Venezuela made him forget.

Watching Angela and Gianni with her nephews and niece, Liliana too imagined Raffaele with a wife and many children. It pained her to think he could look and feel for another woman the way he claimed he could only for her. Of course, he'd moved on and settled down with a beautiful South American goddess. Both Raffaele and Domenico had abandoned her. Stopped loving her. Lied to her.

"Davide is different, I can see it. He's going to be a teacher just like Francesca. Times are different now. Men don't leave for work like they used to."

"No, instead of leaving for work, they leave because of those crazy fascists bombing piazzas and killing people."

"Ma, it's worse in Milano. Davide is from Rome. We can't stop Francesca because we are scared. It's her life. She has to decide, and if I could go back, I would have decided differently too." Liliana sighed. Francesca was more like Angela than her mother. She did as she pleased, managing to stay free from the gossip. Amara's attempts at employing Francesca in the dress shop had failed; she was determined to teach. Unlike her, Francesca would get out of Gildone.

Liliana watched Francesca as she sat on the couch reading. Her hair rest was big and full. She'd put a layer of pink eyeshadow, which accentuated her dark, almost-black eyes. Her legs were curled up underneath her. Her face relaxed and lips were gently curved into a slight smile. Liliana was glad she encouraged her daughter to read. Looking at her engaged in the pages of whatever novel, it was clear her daughter would always find a way to escape these confining stone walls.

#

9 October 1952

My Dearest Liliana,

I thought of you the other day when I walked past the bakery. I am always thinking of you, but the smell of the bread brought me back home. I ended up walking into the bakery on my way back from work and buying three loaves of bread. It's just me in the house. I don't know what I was thinking.

My brother came to visit a few months ago. I finally got to meet my nephew and niece. It was so exciting to meet them. It made me think I should try to visit. I miss our town. Is the bar still so busy? I always enjoyed having a drink there after work and seeing the bus arrive from Campobasso. Did you ever see that bus stop and wonder who might step off of it? We never really had many strangers pass through our town. Is that still the case? How odd it would be for a stranger to pass through our small town. Where do you think he'd go?

When it's not so busy, I'll write again.

Thinking of you.

With all my love,
Raffaele

Chapter 5

Some of the women in town sighted Davide and Francesca holding hands and walking the outer edges of Gildone. The two reminded Liliana of her and Raffaele's days together. Raffaele had asked Senore Farinacci if they could take unchaperoned walks together, and her father had obliged, but because of Angela's growing belly, she and Raffaele usually met away from the center to avoid being seen. Liliana overheard her parents arguing one evening after she'd returned from a date with Raffaele.

"People are going to think we have two daughters who can't stay out of trouble." Her mother was pacing in the kitchen.

"They won't. Lili has never been wild like Angela." He took a puff from his pipe. Smoke circled his face. Liliana stood on the stair trying not to make a sound.

"Well, let's make sure they don't parade across town."

After that she and Raffaele rushed past the center, nodding hello to Senora Pollentino, who crocheted on her balcony. After passing the center, they'd slowly climb the roads that were woven into the side of the mountain. Once they reached the outer edges of Gildone, they held hands and walked back to Liliana's house. It was on her way to the bakery one afternoon that she heard Senore Pollentino whisper to another woman.

"Did you see the older Farinacci girl with Raffaele?"

"That's how it started with the younger one."

"And Amara hasn't even started with the wedding plans for Angela."

"That is why my daughter gets chaperoned"

Cluck.

Cluck.

Cluck.

Even as the years had helped the women to somewhat forget, Liliana taught Francesca to avoid the women in town. Francesca had seen the damage her father's abandonment had done to her mother. Francesca remembered hearing her mother cry at night; her mother thinking Francesca couldn't hear. Liliana pulled away from the women in town, even though there were some who'd been through similar tragedies. Many of those women had been forsaken and pregnant. However, most had moved on. Liliana was unable, worrying too much about what the others might think about how she mothered Francesca. Liliana hadn't told her much about Domenico.

Francesca told Davide of the possible divorce and explained, "I'm nothing like him, you know?" An uncertainty lingered. "How could I be? I've never met him."

Davide looked at his girl; she was broken.

"What do you know about him?"

"My father?" She looked up, then down into the floor. "Not much. I've only seen one picture of him, and it was taken years before he even met my mother."

"So, you don't know anything about him? What about your grandparents?"

"I've never met them. They're not from Gildone. My mother rarely mentions them. She told me my grandmother died when I was younger, and I don't know about my grandfather."

Francesca wondered if her grandparents had heard from her father. Their negligence toward her and Liliana had wounded her mother in a similar way Domenico's abandonment had hurt Liliana.

"My mother even went to her funeral, and there was more gossip than she could handle. She gave up completely after that. She keeps to herself now. She doesn't bother with anyone here. I wish she would move out of this town before it's too late, and she's old and stuck like some of the other women in this damn town."

"I'll take you away from here," he promised.

"I hope so." She sighed. "I hope so."

"Carina, I'm not worried. I never was, I never will be." With that, he took her hands kissed them, then leaned forward to kiss her. "You're going to be a good wife, just like your mom would have been had your father given her the chance."

#

The engagement party was set for February. There they would announce a summer wedding. In June, the farmer's fields would look like a quilt, and the trees and flowers in Gildone would be in blossom. The air would still hint of spring, making it the perfect weather for an outdoor party. Liliana never understood brides who chose to wed in winter. The stones of the town made it even colder, and even the walls of the town couldn't protect anyone from the wind. It was dreadful and often snowed. Liliana was grateful her daughter had chosen to be a June bride. She was eager to marry. Liliana knew Francesca's eagerness was in large part because she would be able to leave Gildone. Still, Liliana couldn't stop thinking about how her marriage was the end of just the two of them. Her baby had grown up. She'd now come home from the bakery and make dinner for just one. She wouldn't hear Francesca open the gate at the bottom of the hill after an evening out with her friends in the town center. With Francesca gone, it would be the way things were right after Domenico left. Though the two of them were rarely loud, with her daughter gone, her house on the hill would be silent. She was relieved Francesca hadn't suffered because of a scandal. She was a good girl. Even Amara could be proud of Francesca. She was smart, beautiful, and most importantly, about to be free.

#

The party for Davide and Francesca was fast approaching. Liliana was eager to prepare a beautiful cake for her daughter. She'd baked cakes for her and Angela's engagement party years ago, and was often asked to bake for such occasions but usually declined because she preferred working with pastries. The other bakery was much more equipped for cakes. She planned the menu for the party when there were lulls at the bakery. Very rarely did customers interrupt her.

"Can I help you?" She loved strangers. They knew nothing of her history, her sadness, the scandals. Only once had she been seduced by a stranger and it had not ended well for her.

When she was younger, Liliana always wanted to meet strangers, which was why she enjoyed running the bakery. When the door opened, she would always wait one second too long to look up or turn around as she hoped she wouldn't recognize the customer. That day when she looked up from the sfogliatelle she was preparing, her breath got caught in her chest. Domenico was handsome and looked like a man from the South. When he smiled, his teeth seemed to emit a beam of twinkling light. He had one dimple on his left cheek. His eyes could have been purple, they were so regal. He was taller than most men, which prevented his uniform from hanging awkwardly off his well-formed body.

He didn't look familiar as he walked through the bakery, causing Liliana to give him attention she usually deprived men of. When she learned who he was, she regretted her flirtatious behavior, but it was too late; he had decided she would be his wife. Domenico, like the rest of Gildone, was aware of Liliana's age and her unfortunate history with Raffaele. Domenico took advantage of her mother's fear. It had been advantageous that Raffaele had been gone for some time. She missed Raffaele terribly but she also wanted to settle down.

Domenico's charm enabled Liliana her to push the memories of Raffaele to the back of her mind. Raffaele had been gone for almost two years, and Liliana had started to forget what his face looked like, how his hair fell, what his voice sounded like. Strangers, they could be dangerous.

"Are you the Liliana Farinacci?" With this question, her mind returned to the bakery, and she realized that her name was spoken outside the stone walls.

"Why do you ask?"

On most occasions, the strangers were former soldiers who fought alongside Domenico. In him, they sought a healing only a brotherhood provided. This boy looked familiar. Her heartbeat quickened. She looked at his face, trying to figure out how he knew her name. Oh God, he could be a son of Raffaele's, maybe even a grandson, his face was so young. Liliana continued to examine his face as he walked around the bakery inspecting the racks of desserts. No, she recognized him from elsewhere.

"A cousin of mine who lives in Ferrazzano mentioned Liliana Farinacci's millefoglie and sfogliatelle were the best. The best in Italy."

"Is your cousin Davide?" She smiled, glad he wasn't related to Raffaele.

"Davide sent me to try them. He can't stop talking about them."

"He's been trying to get me to make them for the engagement party. We will have to see. His flattery might be working."

"Well, may I try them?"

"Of course."

She reached for one of each in the display cases and sprinkled them with powdered sugar. She placed them on a small dish and handed him a napkin. He took the millefoglie first. They were traditional and filled with custard. Although she also had spinach and eggplant, the custard filling that engulfed the bakery with the smell of lemon, vanilla, and sugar were her favorite: the different layers, some crispy, some soft from the custard seeping into them, the perfect combination of textures. He took one bite and dusted sugar on his sharp Roman nose. His eyes closed as if the flavors were washing over him. Liliana knew if he had been standing he would have landed on the floor.

"Oh my, Senora. This is the best."

"Thank you." Her hands, which she had crossed over her chest in defense, began to relax. "Try the sfogliatelle."

"Is it true you can make them without any help?"

"I make them alone, yes. My father taught me how. This was his bakery." Her tongue was suddenly loose, eager to share her story with this young boy. He was charming like Davide. She could see why Francesca was looking forward to being part of their family.

Again, he took a bite. The sound of his teeth breaking through the sugar-covered, crispy outer shell took Liliana out of the bakery. She remembered Raffaele, too, would eat her pastries with gusto, not letting a single crumb escape his lips. She watched as this man, a few years younger than Davide, managed to inhale the cream filling inside the sfogliatelle.

"It's so creamy. I couldn't even tell there was ricotta inside." He took a deep breath. "So good."

Liliana knew this batch of sfogliatelle and millefoglie had turned out well. She could see, as she mixed the two in the large silver mixing bowl, the grainy ricotta blending with sugar and semolina. She whisked the mixture the way her father had taught her; in this way, for a moment, it felt as if he was in the back of the bakery with her. As she watched Davide's younger cousin indulge in the mid-afternoon snack, she almost questioned her initial decision to make the Gateau St. Honore. She had heard about the cake on the radio. Liliana had grown to enjoy shows that distracted her from the news.

"Here." She placed a few pastries in a box for him and tied them with some string. "Take some home."

"Thank you, Senora."

"Will I be seeing you at the engagement party?"

"Yes," he said with a mouthful of pastry.

"Good."

"Will these," he pointed to his empty plate, "be at the party."

"Not this time. I'm making something different. It will be good, though. I promise."

Francesca had been quiet about her disappointment when Liliana announced she'd make a cake instead of the usual pastries, but as usual, her daughter had spared her mother's feelings. Liliana had never baked the cake created by St. Honore, the patron saint of baking, but was sure preparing a cake honoring a saint was likely not to go too terribly. St. Honore would be watching over her as she worked the ingredients. Francesca retrieved the recipe for her mother from a French cookbook at the library. She laid the handwritten instructions on the kitchen table.

"Ma, this looks intense."

"I make sfogliatelle, don't I?"

"The best."

"So, you think I can't handle this cake?"

"I'm just saying you don't have to go crazy." She knew her mother could bake anything; she just didn't want to trouble her. She had seen her mother in her perfectionist state, and it usually ended with spoons, flour, and tears on the floor. "It's not a big deal. The wedding cake is more important. I think…"

"You leave the baking to me, carina."

Francesca had planned to do so; interfering with a project her mother planned usually was a regretful decision. Still, she didn't know how to tell her mother that she really wanted at least millefoglie to be on the dessert menu for both the wedding and the engagement.

For her first communion and confirmation, her mother decided to make a six-layer cake for the whole town. Francesca learned later this project was her mother's attempt at changing her history with them. Liliana wanted to be known for something other than a tragedy. It had been a larger project than she anticipated. Her first batch of icing was too sweet, and the toasted almonds intended to decorate the sides of the cake had been toasted for too long and sliced too thick. The church had asked Liliana to bring the cake the morning of the ceremonies. Francesca remembered Amara warning Liliana.

"If your father was alive to help you, I'd still tell you making this cake was a bad idea."

"I have to do it."

"Well, now you do. The whole town knows about it. They're expecting something wonderful." She sighed. "Farinacci family always find a way to make a spectacle. You're just like your father."

"Okay, so?" She digested what her mother said. "The only reason the town knows about this cake is that you keep blabbing."

"*Me?*"

"Who else?"

"You're nuts."

"Am I? The women keep coming into the bakery. They tell me, 'your mother told us this' and 'she told us that.' You keep your mouth too loose when you're altering their clothes."

Francesca watched her grandmother move her bottom lip up towards the top. Tightening her already thin lips together. Her grandmother looked defeated. Her mother hit a wound, intentionally. Amara looked down as if to look through the floor. Francesca's little fingers held onto the kitchen table where she sat. She remembered how much she missed her grandfather. Senore Farinacci would have prevented this moment and protected the two women from each other.

"Ma." Liliana broke through the quiet. "I'm sorry. It's just this cake and the women."

Francesca watched her aging grandmother get up from the table. Her wrinkled hands gripped the edge of the table as she forced herself up.

"I know. You'll be fine. Soon, when there are other things to talk about, this town will forget this cake. They'll forget you, carina."

Francesca was sure this was exactly what her mother had wanted. She wanted the town to forget that she raised her daughter alone. That she baked to survive. Watching her mother suffer forced her to ignore her natural inclinations towards flavors and food. After her communion, after she committed herself to the church, after they celebrated with the most perfect vanilla cake soaked in rum and filled with chocolate ricotta custard and whipped cream frosting sprinkled with toasted almonds, Francesca realized her mother could do anything.

As Francesca planned the engagement, she worried, as her mother did, about the reaction to the cake and the reaction to her officially leaving Gildone days after the wedding. Francesca worried her grandmother might ask her to hang the bed sheets from her window. Amara tended to be so stuck in the old traditions. She even insisted Francesca move in with Davide's family, as was custom forty years ago in Italy.

"Ma, you don't think she'll ask me to, do you?"

"You never know with her."

"I won't do it. No one does it anymore."

"I know. You won't have to."

"Are you sure?"

"Yes, I'm sure."

"I think you were the last girl to hang them. If it wasn't you, then it was Senore Pollentino's daughter. She was about your age, right?

"Don't remind me." She looked out at the clothesline, remembering the stained sheets: the sheets she had been so desperate to stain with a fingerprint, hoping not to upset anyone. She remembered them hanging from her mother's house. They hung while the whole town looked, hoping to have another reason to gossip and instill shame on a girl who had behaved. The Catholic guilt buried deep and showed so blatantly on the sheets. The morning after her wedding, she let Domenico sleep in. Amara was not pleased. She was eager to show Gildone how she'd been more than able to raise a good Catholic girl. Liliana left him up in the bedroom sleeping, hoping to stall her mother, but when Domenico joined the family in the kitchen, Amara rushed towards the stairs.

"Oh good, I'll get the sheets." She motioned for Liliana to join her.

Liliana had been dreading this moment since the day she knew it would come. She hated making a scene and was sure hanging bloody sheets for all of Gildone to see would do exactly that. Amara looked at her daughter as if having swallowed a bee, and reached for the doorknob. The sheets were still on the bed, and the stain on the fitted sheet was not bold but clear. Her mother's eyes scanned the room. Looking at the clock, she realized she was running late; mass was going to begin in less than two hours. The town would be passing by soon. She pulled the sheets, almost ripping them, and rushed out of the room. Liliana didn't understand why she was even called to the bedroom and stared at the bed. Amara retrieved the sheets and headed towards the balcony. Liliana could hear the metal of the pulley scraping against itself as the stained sheet was moved to the center of the clothing line. She reached for the rest of the sheets and brought them downstairs to be washed. When she returned to the kitchen, she found Angela had arrived and was with their mother talking and laughing.

"Aren't you glad it's over now?" Angela said, her eyes beaming into Liliana. Liliana responded with a shrug. Was it really over? It seemed to have not even begun. The town hadn't seen the sheets, and that was the important part of this ridiculous ritual. She stood on the balcony, feeling heat swell from the stone, through the crowd to her face. They weren't looking at her, just at the sheets, as if the stain had some kind of message in it. There was a hum of voices, not as out-of-sync as the march the day before, but still unintelligible.

"Congratulations, Senore Farinacci!"

"Amara, you must be so proud!"

Liliana wanted to vomit all over them. Why should she be proud? Liliana was the one who had behaved. While everyone shouted, wishing her parents congratulations, Amara had grabbed Liliana's hand, squeezing it in thanks. It didn't matter that just eight hours earlier she been downstairs digging in her mother's sewing basket, searching for a pin, and pricking her fingers so she could defile the white sheets. All they cared about now was that there was indeed a stain and she had, at least according to the sheets, been a virgin. She looked at their artificial smiles and exaggerated congratulations, unaware of the possibility that Liliana and the women who came before her were incapable of fraud. These women, who hung their sheets to prove their innocence, could not have been troubled enough to use a sewing pin. As the people of Gildone rushed to stand underneath the balcony, a hushed excitement could be felt. They had not wanted her to be pure. What would have excited them was not the stained the sheet but the sheet having not been hung. Another scandal proving that the women in the Farinacci family were nothing short of uncontrolled. The men were sending congratulations from down below them while the women stood next to their husbands, unable to find anything to cluck about. Their silence made Liliana a lion. She stood proudly, knowing they could say nothing about her. They couldn't say she had been wild like Angela or foolish as she had been in her Raffaele days. She, instead, had done well by her family, and in this small town, that was all they cared about.

Though it was obvious the ritual coerced girls tempted by the desire to think twice, it didn't stop the act from happening. It instead forced them to feel shame. For Liliana, being a woman in Gildone came with the constant fear that she could do nothing right. Even though she'd behaved, all that mattered to Amara was that she had proof she'd done well raising at least one daughter. But Liliana knew she'd done well with Francesca, and no tribal ritual was necessary. It was just a big act that used props.

"I'm so grateful it's a ritual that is out of style," Liliana whispered to herself.

Francesca smiled at her mother's insisting she would not have to be shamed in front of the town. She had waited to be with Davide, afraid the Catholic secret service would find out if she had sinned. She also wanted to give Davide what the priest, her mother, and Catholic teachings described as the most precious gift a wife could provide a husband: her purity. She was glad she waited; there was no hurry. Not to mention waiting was full proof against pregnancy, and the Farinacci women were obviously quite good at that. Waiting and behaving, she and modern science knew, would not guarantee any staining. The idea was medieval. Francesca imagined how embarrassing it must have been for all those women. That feeling of waking up the morning after being with their husbands for the first time and searching for a small dot of blood. Going from a sweet, blushing bride, to the hysterical woman, fearing she might disgrace her family and embarrass her husband, and all over something as inane as this primitive ritual. Her whole life Francesca had been told she was nothing like her mother. She looked nothing like her, and goodness knows, she didn't worry about the thoughts of each and every person in Gildone. Unlike her mother, she would adopt her husband's last name; she would be Mrs. Davide Amato. Though she was glad she was Francesca Farinacci and not Francesca Cappelino. She was a Farinacci, after all. Just like her mother.

#

11 December 1952

My Dearest Liliana,

I've saved up quite a bit and bought a little house for us. It has a yard for a garden, and it's close to the church. In a few months, I'll send you the money so you can buy fare for the ride here. I am a bit worried about sending over the money since I haven't heard from, but I won't rest until I can wake up next to you.

Some days I think I need to save up more so I can come and get you in person. I just don't think it would be smart to leave the business for that long. I just can't help but worry that you've moved on. Why have you been so quiet?

I'll write soon.

With all my love,
Raffaele

Chapter 6

The engagement went smoothly. The snow melted, revealing a mountainside of green, yellow, and orange. The trees began to bud, and the melancholy that sometimes stuck around because of winter had ceased. Francesca decided on having the wedding in Campobasso, a more central location. It would not be a small affair like Domenico and Liliana's wedding. It pleased Liliana to see her daughter so happy. From the day she realized she was going to have a child, all she wanted was to know she'd be able to see her child content.

For the wedding, Francesca demanded a dress made from silk; the color not completely white.

"Absolutely, not!" Amara exclaimed when she saw the dress Francesca stood in.

"Nonna, it's perfect. I love it. I don't look good in white."

Amara turned to Liliana, her eyes pleaded.

Liliana looked at her mother and shrugged. Francesca stood in the mirror staring at herself in the dress. She looked radiant. Her smile was wide and her dimples visible.

"Nonna, times are different now," Francesca said. "No one cares. Honestly, you and momma are so alike. Always worried about everyone except yourselves."

Amara walked over to her granddaughter running her hands on the delicate fabric.

"Well, we need to take it in here." She began to pin the sides of the dress. "If you have a figure like this, you should show it off." Amara looked back at Liliana.

"Thank you," Liliana mouthed to her mother.

"You'll see, Nonna. No one will be talking about the color of the dress. They'll just be talking about how Mamma didn't make any sfogiatelle." She winked at her mother and started to laugh.

Francesca was relieved the issue of the dress had been tabled. Her whole life Liliana tried to protect Francesca from the pecking and clawing she had faced at Francesca's age. When she and her mother would walk back from church sometimes, and the weather was nice, her mother would light a cigarette when the reached the edge of the town center and tell her about some of the snarky remarks and comments about being a single mother. Though her mother never said it outright, her mother could have used a friend. It made Francesca angry to see these women working against each other instead of with each other. The women appeared to be too absorbed with the men in their lives to realize how important they were to each other. Francesca couldn't understand why they didn't support each other. They, too, had husbands they missed. Francesca wanted to see them gather around each other, holding one another up. Francesca watched Angela hold her mother when she needed it. Thinking of these moments between her mother and her aunt made her wish she, too, could have a sister. Though her cousins were the closest thing to sisters that she would ever have, it was not the same. Francesca learned the different strengths a woman could possess through her grandmother, her mother, and her aunt. She was glad she stood her ground regarding the silk dress. There was only shame in not wearing white if the right to wear it had not been earned. Francesca knew she was pure, as did Davide and God, and to her, that was all that mattered.

#

Before Francesca could stop to digest a moment or a slice of her mother's perfect vanilla and strawberry cake, the wedding was over. She and Davide spent two weeks in a small hotel in Capri for their honeymoon. They left their room only for food and a quick evening walk past the high-end shops. In Capri, they could forget that their jobs and the new apartment waited for them. They returned to Campobasso and prepared for the beginning of their first year of teaching and their marriage.

#

Coming home to Davide, who sat at their kitchen table grading papers, always put a smile on Francesca's face. He sat with his feet grounded firmly to the kitchen floor and his red pencil held prisoner between his teeth and lips. She interrupted his intensity, placing bags from the market next to his "to be graded" pile. He was so organized when he worked, which surprised her; he was always late and frazzled all the time. She graded papers with a system she had perfected.

"I can't understand it. You've got papers all over the place. It makes no sense. I thought you were the organized one." He pushed aside her papers to make room for the groceries.

"Yeah, so."

"It's a miracle you don't lose anything." He continued.

"When I do, I pray to Saint Anthony. I always find whatever I'm looking for."

Davide knew well Francesca's dependence on St. Anthony. She could be found most Saturdays cleaning and muttering to herself, "St. Anthony, help me."

At the start of their marriage, this was their quiet routine teach, eat, and clean. Most days Francesca would enter the kitchen, bags of fresh produce on the table, intruding on Davide's focus. It took a month or two for Davide to accept that she was not going to change the kitchen table mess habit. The two were content in their small walking distance from their work to their apartment. It was a quiet existence, especially during the school year. Though Francesca had what she always desired, a husband who loved her and freedom from Gildone's stone walls, sometimes she wondered if there was more out there for her, for them. Maybe it was time for a baby.

During summer visits to Gildone, Francesca watched her mother, aunt, and grandmother age. Francesca could see her mother felt fine, even though Liliana only saw her and Davide once a week if that. Each time she went to see her mother she hoped to see her mother free from the pain she carried. Especially now that Liliana's one reminder that she and Domenico had been together no longer lived in her house. Francesca had moved on, accepting that she would never know her father, and she wished the same for her mother. Each visit, be it a Sunday or all of summer, the three would interrogate Francesca. They often sat at Amara's kitchen table, espressos in hand.

"Well, aren't you trying to have a baby?"

"Yes, Nonna." She blushed, knowing her grandmother would know what happened behind the closed door of her and Davide's bedroom.

"Well, where is this baby, then?" she prodded.

"You two have been married four years this June."

"Thank you, Mother. I am aware."

"Leave her alone." Zia Angela always took her side.

"You're only being nice to her because you get to bug your daughters. You've gotten your fix."

"Okay. So?"

"How about I have this baby when He," she pointed upwards, "thinks I'm ready."

She and Davide had been trying and trying. Every Sunday, at mass, they both lit a candle to Saint Anne, hoping to conceive. Each time her cycle began, she knew she and Davide's routine would remain unchanged. Another evening would pass as she made lentil soup, serving it to him, unable to find comfort in the aroma knowing she could not break any good news. For four years, each day had been the same. Delightful, but uninterrupted.

#

10 *May 1953*

My Dearest Liliana,

Did you receive my last letter? It surprised me that you hadn't written back since I finally called for you. Every day I walk to the mailbox hoping to see a letter from you, but still, I wait.

I asked Tonino if he had heard anything, but he says he hasn't. I hope all is well with you and to hear from you soon.

With all my love,
Raffaele

Chapter 7

Francesca knew within an instant she and Davide had finally conceived on an unusually cold May evening. She lay in the bed, naked between the sheets.

"How can you tell?" Davide's hand caressed her nude back.

"It felt perfect."

She continued to repeat "perfect" and with a gentle touch rubbed her belly.

"I think you're right."

She woke up feeling changed. After a few weeks, she struggled to wake for work. She was so fatigued. She wondered if perhaps there might finally be a little baby growing inside her. She pushed the thought away not wanting to get her hopes up. She knew for certain when she and Davide returned from a Sunday visit in Gildone. She walked from the bus stop, passing the few churchgoers.

"Francesca?" Senora Pollentina called out.

"Hi." She resisted rolling her eyes.

"It's been so long. How's the married life? Campobasso?" the Senora asked.

"It's good." She looked at Davide, whose hand rested on the small of her back. She knew the senora would run back to the other mothers, telling them she'd spoken with Liliana's daughter. She revealed nothing to her.

"You look different."

"Well, I am getting older."

"No, it's something else." The Senora smiled, not saying anything else.

"Well, I better be going. They've probably thrown the pasta. You know how it is." Francesca smiled and nodded. She grabbed Davide's hand, leading him toward Amara's house.

They arrived to an empty house.

"They must be at my mother's." Francesca remembered her mother had mentioned how Nonna Amara was doing too much and getting tired. The turned around and walked over to her grandmother's house.

They entered.

"*Permesso?*"

"*Entrada,*" the women, Giacomo, and Gianni replied.

The smell of her mother's Bolognese took over Francesca. She wanted to eat. The browned ground meat, onions, and ripe garden tomatoes were the only thoughts in Francesca's mind. Her pupils dilated when she saw her aunt had prepared chicken marsala. The mushrooms glistened.

While the women picked up the dishes after the first course, they huddled in Liliana's small kitchen.

"You look different," Amara noticed.

"Oh, brother," Francesca and Zia Angela replied.

"You do."

"Senora Pollentino stopped me in the center and told me the same thing."

The women looked at each other, encircled Francesca, and embraced her. She had not been told that Senora Pollentino had predicted and been correct about almost all the women in Gildone being pregnant. The woman could smell a pregnancy days after conception. She said she could see it from the way a woman's eyes seemed softer once she was with child.

"*What?* Ugh! Get off."

Laughing, they backed away from her.

"I could see it when you walked in the door."

"How?"

"I looked the same when I was pregnant with you."

"She did," Angela agreed.

Liliana remembered how her hair had never looked healthier, the natural glow so bright she could have been mistaken for a Greek Goddess. She also looked tired, but in a way that hadn't indicated stress, but of something growing. She was a beautiful pregnant woman, and her daughter was even more so.

"Did you take a pregnancy test?" Amara asked.

"No, not yet. I guess I'll have to take one tomorrow."

"Oh, you know she is. Just look at her," Angela said.

They collected the second-course dishes, giggling and looking at Francesca.

"What is all the laughing about? Davide asked. The women looked at each other and laughed. Francesca would take a test after work and tell him.

#

The day the baby arrived was the coldest day February would bring: the sky a clear blue and the sun a ball of ice glistening. The warmest place in Gildone was near the vent that released the warm air from the bakery, making the whole town smell like bread. Francesca had prepared for the baby to be born at a hospital, alongside a doctor, but her mid-week visit to her mother's ended with her delivering in her former bedroom. The air that day was biting cold, and for Francesca, the walk from the bus stop to her mother's was what induced the baby's arrival. Davide arrived on the last bus of the evening, his hair was disheveled and eyes excited. As he exited the bus, he dropped his school bag and a stack of papers. He knocked on Liliana's door in a near panic. Amara opened the door, raising her rough hands to her lips.

"She's sleeping, and so is the baby."

"Is everyone okay?"

"The baby is fine, but Francesca isn't doing great. The doctor says she needs her rest."

"May I see the baby?"

Amara led him up the stairs; her old feet and ever-growing hips did not make a sound going up.

"Francesca wants to name her Anna."

"Anna." He smiled as he looked at his baby girl. "She's perfect."

Amara watched as Davide picked up his new daughter. She looked even smaller in his hands. The room was filled with all the little newborns, and there stood Davide with his daughter as if it were just the two of them.

"Anna, carina, Anna," he repeated to his little girl.

When Anna began to fuss, he handed her to Amara. She led him to Francesca's room. She stopped in front of the door and whispered to Davide.

"She didn't want to hold the baby. She looked at her, cried, then asked us to go wash her. Davide." She put her hand on his forearm. "I'm a bit worried."

#

Months passed before Francesca felt comfortable holding Anna. Francesca would hear Anna crying from the nursery, and try to ignore it. She knew Anna needed to be fed, but the thought of nursing her baby was all too difficult. It didn't help that Francesca hadn't slept since before she was pregnant. Still, it impossible to ignore her crying baby, and so she dragged her slippered feet to Anna's room and sit in the rocking chair still unable to pick Anna up. When the wailing became unbearable, she'd pick Anna up and try to nurse her. The baby would look up at her with relief while she fed. Francesca would look away and stare out of the window. Tears streaming down her face.

The shock of motherhood and the thought of her baby girl not being safe caused Francesca's heart to knock hard in her chest. She constantly worried about Anna's safety and at times her thoughts made it difficult to breathe. She couldn't keep her baby safe. No one could. She'd put Anna back in her bassinet after she fed or changed her, but still, the wailing wouldn't cease. Anna was a fussy baby. Davide returned from work often finding his wife sobbing in the living room while his daughter screamed with her little mouth wide open and face red with fear and hunger. Motherhood was going to break Francesca. She was sure of it.

"She's making Davide and me crazy. What can I do?" Francesca needed air. "Ma, she doesn't have a fever, I've changed her, fed her, and burped her." She groaned and ran her hands through her hair. "She's not teething. What is it? I can't take it." She held Anna as the baby continued to wail.

Liliana looked at Angela. They both then looked at Amara.

"You think?" Angela asked her mother. She looked at Amara and knew.

"It has to be *oo malocchio*," Amara explained.

Francesca, too, had been a victim of the *malocchio* as a child. It seemed many of her first memories involved her mother, aunt, and grandmother gathered around a table chanting.

Amara stood up and nodded. Francesca watched her grandmother head to her bedroom where she kept the holy water.

Angela, Liliana, and Francesca took turns holding the baby as she continued to scream. When Amara returned, she retrieved three clean bowls from the cupboards, a spoon, and some olive oil. They sat down at the table. Angela, closest to Amara, held Anna, who, although exhausted, continued to cry. Anna's face was crinkled and red. She cried with her mouth wide open, revealing no teeth, only a little baby tongue.

Amara filled the three bowls with holy water. Her face was serious. Liliana had watched her mother do this many times before; she knew only the procedures, not the chants. Francesca shifted uneasily in her seat; the rite they performed made her uncomfortable. She would likely need to go to confession after this. The women knew the church would not approve of this ritual. Still, they practiced it. It always came with remarkable success, and so the Farinacci women, along with many other women in the small villages of Italy, practiced the *malocchio* ritual behind closed doors, protected by a crucifix.

Amara poured the olive oil into the spoon and rested the spoon on the edge of the bowl, careful not to drip the oil into the bowl. Then she began with the sign of the cross.

"In the name of the father, the son, and the Holy Spirit," her voice carried across the room. The other three women did the same, kissing their hands when finished. Amara then did another sign of the cross, this time over the water, chanting under her breath. She did this three times, then dipped her finger in the olive oil.

Francesca watched, trying to hear her grandmother. It worked best in silence, but baby Anna continued to scream. Her little lungs tried to take in more air so she could wail. Although Francesca didn't completely approve of the ritual, she wanted to learn should she need to remove the *malocchio* from Anna again. But she couldn't hear her grandmother and would have to wait until Angela decided to teach it to her. Only her aunt had been taught the ritual. Amara placed her thumb on Anna's forehead, making a sign of the cross the same way a priest anoints the sick. She chanted again, something different, three times. Francesca heard the last of the chant, catching "*chicte la date.*" The words upset her as she thought of all the people who had approached her at mass, complimenting Anna on her beauty. She should have known better. She would need to add a gold *chornico* charm next to the crucifix that rest on Anna's neck.

Amara dipped her finger in the oil once more, this time letting the oil drop into the water. The women leaned forward, eager to see if the oil would dilute into the water.

Francesca's eyes widened as the oil spread out, creating an iridescent sheen over the water. Angela placed her hand on the baby to calm her. Francesca looked at her grandmother who was not surprised to see the oil and water melt into each other. Liliana took Francesca's hand into hers and gave it a squeeze she didn't realize she needed.

"Oh no," Francesca whispered.

"It'll be fine, Nonna Amara will take care of it."

"Francesca," Amara warned, her beady eyes piercing her granddaughter, "you must be more careful."

"She didn't realize," Angela reminded her mother.

Francesca had not realized how often the townspeople had caressed, held, and complemented the baby. They had tempted the Fates. Sure, Amara had warned Francesca early on that complimenting and commenting on how beautiful a baby though seemingly innocent could be a sign of jealousy, but Francesca didn't believe it was that serious.

"They say these nice things like, 'She's so beautiful. You're so lucky,' but in their heart, they wish they could have a beautiful daughter or granddaughter. This is how the *malocchio* works."

Her grandmother continued, "That's why when someone says something nice about the baby, and especially if they touch the baby, while they say it, you need to say, 'God bless' afterward. It helps protect the baby."

Again, Amara repeated the ritual, each time the oil diluted less and less. The last time, she pressed the oil onto Anna's forehead, she watched the baby close her eyes. Angela handed the baby to Francesca. She looked down at Anna. Her little head pressed against Francesca's chest and her hands wrapped themselves so tight around Francesca's they looked white. Francesca took in a calming breath. Her baby blues had passed. She had been thrown into motherhood, and the adjustment period was over, for now.

#

Amara left after the baby rested in her crib. Liliana returned to the bakery to prepare for the dinner rush. Amara picked up some bread then headed to her house, passing the church on the way. As she looked up at the modest stone tower and heavy doors, she thought on the day's events. Though Francesca hadn't suffered in the same way Liliana had, motherhood was turning out to be very hard on her granddaughter. Deciding she wanted to go inside the church, Amara pushed the heavy doors open. She sat at the back of the church and began to say a prayer of thanks that her great-grandbaby was calm and resting. As she began to pray and think of some of the turbulent times her daughters and now granddaughter were going through, she thought of the thirty-year secret fastened by red satin. She stood up from the pew and entered the confessional, bread and all.

"Bless me, Father, for I have sinned. It has been three decades since my last confession."

"Three decades. What weight have you decided to lift, my child?"

She told the priest about the letters that came for so many years after Raffaele had left, her daughter's sadness, and Domenico's abandonment.

"Haven't I stolen her chance to be happy?" she nearly shouted, unable to control her fear and guilt. "If I tell her, won't it kill her?"

She listened, nodded her head, and gently wiped her tears. As the priest spoke, she thought about how lonely Liliana's life had turned out. She had prevented Raffaele and Liliana from being together. She worried he wouldn't have been enough for her daughter the way Franco was for her. After what happened with Angela, she couldn't bear seeing another one of her daughters be the topic of the town's gossip. This was why she encouraged Liliana to marry Domenico. He was a soldier. He was handsome. He was successful. All those years she had pushed her daughter away from Raffaele, and he clearly loved her. Amara couldn't say the same for Domenico, especially not after Domenico's silence all these years. She wanted someone like Franco for her daughters, and while Angela's family life turned out fine with beautiful children and a loving husband, Liliana's life was a lonely one. Amara couldn't help but think she had been a horrible mother to Liliana. The priest finished.

"Child, telling your daughter is the only way to be free of this burden. Then you must ask and wait for her forgiveness." He gave her a penance. She left the church, her heart heavier with guilt.

Chapter 8

Because Amara lived alone, Angela, Gianni, and Liliana met at her house for supper. They took turns cooking, though Amara usually took over. She didn't love food the way her husband had, and the way Liliana and Francesca did. She prepared food in a simple way. For her food was nourishment, not a source of pleasure. That evening she prepared *rapini*, sausage, and garlic served over *orecchiette*. It was a recipe from Bari, and all of Italy acknowledged that the Baresse knew their way around the kitchen. Liliana entered the house, the strong smell of garlic and wine entered her nostrils. She carried a box of biscotti for her mother to have for breakfast.

"Hey, Ma." She startled her mother. Amara stood watching the pot of water, thinking of her penance.

"You scared me."

"Sorry." Liliana reached for the dishes and began setting the table as she had for so many years in that kitchen before she married. Years had passed, and not much changed for Liliana. She still ran the bakery. She was still alone and still ate dinner with her mother and sister. The only changes she noticed were their looks. The women nearly stopped gossiping about her, Domenico and Raffaele. Liliana had always been voluptuous but now carried more weight in her hips and chest, and the women weren't afraid to mention it. Her hands revealed both her profession and her age. She had aged more quickly than her sister.

Amara, too, looked older. Her olive skin revealed spots around her eyes no cream or procedure would remove. And her bun, though mostly black, revealed some gray and white hairs. Most of the change in her mother, Liliana realized, was how she carried her shoulders as if transporting large bags of flour.

Angela entered the kitchen as her mother and sister both sat down. She joined them at the table.

"Gianni will be right in." She felt the temperature change in the room. The air was dense and cool, a storm was on its way. "Is everything okay?" She looked past the two of them and out towards the summer sun as it set, making the mountainside seem painted by a sheer orange lacquer. Her mother sat upright. She leaned forward, away from the back of the chair. Her arms rested in her lap. Angela mirrored their mother only her head was tilted upward at Liliana. Angela blinked in quick succession.

"We're just tired," Amara spoke for the two of them.

Angela turned to her mother, her eyes darting up and down. Amara didn't move. Angela looked down at her hands. She put her hands together and twiddled her thumbs. Liliana could see specks of dust floating in the air, illuminated by the setting sun.

"I'm starving. Let's eat!" Gianni said. His face had tanned from the field. He entered, breaking the tension. Amara, Liliana, and Angela served dinner. The women listened as Gianni told them about the harvest. It was a quiet meal.

Liliana left after the table had been cleared, and Gianni left soon after, both needing to rest since they woke early for work. When she heard the screen door close, announcing Gianni's exit, Amara pulled Angela to the kitchen table. She handed her an espresso and poured a short cup for herself. Amara put the cup down onto the table. Taking the edge of the table cloth into her hands, which revealed a slight tremor, she gently folded it. She took the cup of espresso placing it down onto the folded tablecloth. With a teaspoon and light touch, she stirred the coffee. The cream that rose to the top blended into the espresso. She put the cup to her lips but stopped before taking a sip.

"I went to confession today." Amara's thoughts flashed back to the confessional. She could see the bread resting on her lap and the silhouette of the priest on the other side of the confession box. Sitting here with Angela she once again she was seeking some kind of reconciliation. Her eyes met with Angela's then darted back to her drink.

"Oh?" Amara looked back at her daughter. Her shoulders nearly touched her ears. Angela leaned forward.

"I did something terrible."

"What are you talking about?" Angela tilted her head and pursed her lips.

Amara stirred the coffee again, picked up the tiny cup, and this time took a small sip. She could feel the coffee on the outer edges of her tongue. She bit her bottom lip in defeat. Amara was not one to admit a fault. She had always put her family first. She wanted only to protect them. There was nothing wrong with her intentions. Still, Amara was struggling to say, once again, what terrible thing she had done to Liliana.

"I know it would turn out this way…" Amara's shook as it trailed off. Her daughter sat silent, waiting to let her finish. "How could I have known?" She was thinking aloud and to no one. She hoped God was listening.

Angela had not broken her stare. Amara could see her daughter taking big breaths. Her chest rising and falling to a steady tempo. Amara, too, took in a deep breath. She began speaking through the exhale.

"The day Liliana was married, a letter arrived for her." She stood up and moved across the kitchen toward the locked drawer where she kept them. Amara stared at the drawer as if her mind could open it. Angela's eyes followed her mother. She retrieved them, returning to the table. It had been years since she held the letters, always in a hurry to hide them. "The letter was from Raffaele. He asked her to respond as quickly as possible if she wanted to marry him and start a life in Venezuela." At the mention of Raffaele, Angela's eyes widened. Amara looked away from her daughter. She pushed her feet into the floor and shifted her weight in the chair.

"Does Lili know?"

"I never told her. I didn't want her to leave," she admitted. "Domenico seemed to be a good man. He had served in the war, had a pension on the way. He told your father and me, he would take good care of her." She remembered how adamant he had been about Liliana. His charming smile disarmed she and her husband. She continued, "Liliana was getting old. I worried she might never marry. It would have been embarrassing for Liliana *and* the family." Amara's voice shook. She pushed a breath out through her nose. "I didn't want another scandal. Her leaving alone to follow Raffaele… how ridiculous would that have been?" She asked no one. She shook her head and was brought back to the kitchen. "It would have been too much."

"Ma, you know how much she loved him. Why?" Angela broke her stare and stood up. She walked closer to her mother. She put her hands in her laps and crossed her ankles. Her shoulders were hunched forward. "I can't believe you haven't told her. After all these years…" She touched the letters. "These are all from him?" Years of love and patience rested on the table, yellowed.

"He wrote to her for years. Years after Domenico left." She took another sip of coffee to clear her throat. "I didn't show her because I couldn't stand to see her in any more pain. I didn't realize he loved her the way he did."

"Did Daddy know?" Angela held her espresso and dropped two teaspoons of sugar in it. She stirred it longer than necessary.

"Of course not. He would have shown her on the wedding day. You know those two were close."

"You have to tell her." Angela took another sip of her coffee. Amara looked at her daughter and shook her head. A strand of her black her slipped over her eyes. She brushed it back.

"What good will it do? Have you been watching her since Francesca left? She looks like she could crack from the pain."

Angela nodded.

"Still, Ma. You need to tell her. It's not right."

Amara closed her eyes. "I'll tell her when I'm ready."

"Ma, it's been over thirty years. Lili's a grandmother. She needs closure. Don't you think she deserves to know? She--"

"Please Angela," Amara interrupted. "I know you two are close, but it will kill me if she hated me." She took a dramatic breath. "I'll die."

Amara, though sincere in her fears, still knew Angela would protect her. Every daughter—in the end—needs her mother.

Chapter 9

"I got the job in Rome." He said it quick as if picking up a hot plate, only to put it back down.

Francesca looked up at him from the book she was reading.

"I know you like living near your mom, but this is a great job. It pays almost double. We'd be foolish not to, and Anna barely knows my parents." He took a deep breath. "The rioting has died down." Another breath. "Francesca, you're going to love Rome."

At first, Francesca struggled with baby Anna, but after learning how to relieve her daughter and self from the *malocchio* and to trust herself as a mother, life with an infant became easier. It had taken some time for Francesca to *want* to pick up baby Anna and cuddle her, but as her anxious feelings faded, she was surprised how much she enjoyed staying home with Anna. After she was born, the doctor informed Francesca that if she ever got pregnant again it would likely kill her, so the dream of having four children ended. Anna was it. The same way Francesca had been for her mother. With each Sunday visit, her mother's loneliness was more visible. She would sit quietly at the end of the table watching everyone eat. Her goodbye-hugs always lingered as they stood to embrace each other in the doorway. She dreaded telling her mother she would be living a bus and train ride away. She knew her mother would worry about the tensions, and not being available to help. Still, she and Davide weren't leaving the country. Francesca would still see her mother for holidays and summers. She also worried about Anna's reaction. Anna, already six, had grown attached to her grandmother who baked her treats and took her to mass. She also loved her great-aunt Angela whose daughters always brought her beautiful handmade dresses lined with precious lace and luxurious ribbons. Dresses she wore proudly to mass.

"Nonna Liliana," Anna began, a sadness lingering in the tone, "can I come to see you?"

"Of course. Promise you'll come every summer."

"I promise."

And with that, the move was settled for Anna. They prearranged dates to learn to bake and cook. Anna smiled a heartsick smile which Liliana returned. Liliana watched Anna's little feet run to tell her mother about their future plans to bake.

"Ma, it's going to be okay. We're still going to see you," Francesca promised as she entered the kitchen.

"I know, carina. I know." Her shoulders dropped. She took a seat at the table. She placed the table cloth in her hands and folded the edge of the fabric and smoothed it with her hands. Liliana looked up at Francesca. "It's for the best. Rome will be good for you three. There are good schools for Anna and you'll be closer to Davide's family."

"I knew you would understand, Ma." Francesca turned toward Anna and motioned for her to get her toys together. She put her hand on her mother's back and gave the top her shoulder a gentle squeeze.

Liliana didn't have the strength to tell Anna or Francesca that their leaving would make her truly alone. She knew what it was like to have a mother who tried to control every choice, and though she might have been able to convince Francesca to stay, it would have been wrong. This is what she wanted for her daughter even at the cost of her own happiness. Motherhood was complicated in this way. She watched as Francesca and Anna prepared to leave and though they weren't leaving for Rome just yet, her chest filled with the same pain she'd felt when her father died. When Domenico left. When Raffaele left. She felt hollow.

Sure, she had Angela and Amara, but for Liliana, her daughter and granddaughter were the egg to her flour; they held her together. Liliana could not understand why the people she loved were always leaving her.

#

The first few summers Francesca hadn't noticed her mother's aging hands and leathered skin. She didn't notice that the dreamy look when she baked had been replaced by a deep dark wondering. Francesca only noticed Gildone had not changed. Yes, there were fewer people living in the village; most had left for Campobasso, America, Argentina, and of course, Venezuela. Still, it was the same; every evening the elderly men sat on the bench by the bus stop. The middle-aged men drank at the bar before seeing their wives who had prepared dinner. There were some children who, like Anna, ran around the village playing and laughing and scraping their knees on the cobblestone. Her mother still made them biscotti brutti, and hid her cigarette habit from the town; as if they hadn't noticed the wrinkles that had formed around her lips. She also noticed in those passing summers how her grandmother had gotten older and Angela aged with grace. It was Angela's the lack of concern for what others thought, a lesson she weathered when she became pregnant with Giacomo that made her so beautiful. Though it was evident Angela and Amara were mother and daughter, her grandmother had a darkness about her, and because of this, the resemblance between Liliana and Amara grew stronger as the years passed.

Anna looked more and more like Davide as she grew. Her fair freckled skin and blond, almost gold hair reminded the few old enough to remember Liliana as a child. Anna and her grandmother had the same mannerisms: the hands on the hips, the crinkled nose when they smiled, and lips that pursed when trying to think of something nice to say. They also both shared an innate need to please.

"Nonna, would it make you happy if I made this with you?"

Francesca watched her mother smile at Anna and nod. For a moment, Francesca remembered her grandfather teaching her to bake, but when he got sick, he stopped. She looked at her mother whose hands were crossed over her chest. Francesca recalled how much she enjoyed baking with her grandfather. The memories like vague, fading snapshots of his big, over-worked hands delicately shaping a small shell of dough. Now that she was older, she wished she knew how to make pastries and bread like her mother. She was so glad Liliana and Anna baked together at their special hideaway, the bakery.

When Francesca arrived with Anna for their summer visits, her mother would be sure to

have a special baking project for the two of them. As Anna got older, Lilianna challenged her.

"This week we are going to work on braiding the rye loaves." They would work and work until Anna could do it almost as well as Liliana. Now, that Anna was almost a teenager she really pushed her.

"This summer we are going to learn to whip a meringue. Nonna is getting old and this always makes her so tired. You're young, carina, it will be easy for you."

Francesca noticed how her mother looked older and tired. Maybe it was from smoking, but her mother had also never let herself move on from Domenico's betrayal. Her mother had embraced her sad existence as destiny. The fates had decided it all for her. All those years of being alone and empty showed in the wrinkles around her mouth and eyes. Her wavy, golden brown hair now beginning to show flecks of grey. Francesca couldn't understand why her mother wouldn't let her father go. Sure, Liliana had loved Domenico, and his leaving and remarrying was a scab that refused to heal, a kind of hemophilia. Francesca knew her mother needed more to survive than affections from Francesca and Anna. Francesca watched as her mother thrived in the summer. Francesca wondered how her mother made it through the harsh Gildonese winter.

Chapter 10

When the priest excused Amara of her sin, of her intrusion on her daughter's fate, he assumed she would rush to release herself of the heavy secret she carried. He was not aware that she would continue to carry the secret and hide the letters. So, when she collapsed on the kitchen floor preparing the most creamy risotto, it came as a surprise to him. Amara asked for Father Miguel, not the doctor. Liliana found her; her eyes staring at the ceiling. Tears rolled down her old skin, moving through the wrinkles of her face, then behind her ears.

"Go get Father Miguel."

"Let me get the doctor first."

"No!" This took all her energy. "Father Miguel."

Liliana ran to the church, passing Francesca, who had closed up the bakery.

"Go get the doctor."

Liliana spoke to the priest while Francesca looked for the doctor.

"Father, I know why this happened." Amara reached for the priest with her withered hands.

"Why?"

"I never told her. Almost seven years have passed since I confessed to you and still…"

"You know what you must do." He placed his soft warm hands on her forehead, whispering a prayer only God could hear. As he finished, the doctor arrived. Amara refused to see him.

"Ma, please let him examine you," Liliana begged.

"I'm fine."

"We should take you to the hospital," Francesca suggested.

"Leave me. I want to rest." A deep sigh. "Please someone clean that pot, I'm sure I burned the bottom of it." She looked at the doctor. "I've had those since I got married."

"Just let him take a look." Angela entered the bedroom, holding Anna's hand.

Amara asked everyone but Angela to leave. Liliana left with Anna as Angela sat on her old bed.

"Angela, I need to tell her."

"I know, Mamma."

"I won't be able to go in peace if I don't." Angela nodded. The priest recognized the speech; like most in her condition, she knew her time was limited.

"Go and get her."

Amara and Liliana were the only two in the room. Anna begged to stay with her grandmother, but Francesca took her down the stairs and made her *zambagolie*.

"Zia Angela, do you know what that's all about?"

She nodded. She wanted to lie, but lies had started this mess.

"Tell me."

It wasn't her place to tell Francesca the details of her sister's love life. It was not her story, but Liliana's. Angela was not surprised that her mother had kept the letters a secret for this long. Her mother was always trying to quell the turmoil and avoid a spectacle. She clearly thought hiding Raffaele's letters was the right move. All these years she'd watched her sister suffer in loneliness, and now she'd feel betrayed by both her mother and sister. Angela looked at her niece. It amazed Angela that even though Francesca had been around her sister's ever-fermenting bitterness, Francesca had found happiness. Angela knew Francesca was not completely aware of her mother's sorrow and now wasn't the time to start explaining.

"I can't."

"But…"

"It isn't my place."

Angela looked at the closed bedroom door. She couldn't hear anything but the hum of the refrigerator and the wind rustling the leaves outside.

Liliana stood in the doorway, her hands on her hips, looking at her mother. Amara was propped up by some pillows. Rosary beads rest in her hands. Her crooked fingers clutched the crucifix. Her mother, whom Liliana perceived as more often than not fierce and unbreakable, now looked weak and small.

Liliana sat next to her mother.

Amara reached out to Liliana, the rosary beads dangled from one hand.

"What is it, Ma?"

"Lili, for a long while, I've been wanting to tell you this, but it never seemed to be the right time?"

"What?

Her mother sat in silence. Liliana could hear birds chirping outside. The wind moved through the trees as if to shush the town. Amara looked away from her daughter, down at the rosary beads, then back up at Liliana. Another gust, louder this time, moved through the leaves outside.

"The day you married Domenico you received a letter."

Liliana's eyes met her mother's. Her heart began to throb in her temples. She put her hand to her forehead.

"It was from Raffaele."

"How?" Liliana struggled to find her breath. "W-w-what?" The room felt smaller than it had moments ago.

"The letter said he was—"Amara coughed. "He was calling for you to go to Venezuela."

Liliana stood up and crossed her hands over her chest. She paced across the floor and stopped at the bed. Her mother centimeters away. Liliana's eyes bore into the floor. She looked up at her mother and felt a fire rising from the belly through her throat and out of her ears. She leaned in. Liliana's face so close to Amara's her nose just about touched her mother's.

She spoke in soft, slow almost-whisper. "I don't believe you."

It couldn't be. It just couldn't. She looked away from her mother. First, she thought Raffaele had abandoned her. That he, like so many of the other men, had forgotten her after stepping foot in Venezuela. Then when it happened again with Domenico, being forsaken was clearly her destiny. First Raffaele then Domenico. It made sense. She was meant to be alone. Now, thirty years later her mother was telling her everything she'd ever thought about how things were supposed to turn out was wrong.

"Lili, I just—"

She put her hand up as if to stop her mother from speaking. None of this made sense. If Raffaele had written she would have known about it.

"You didn't…. "She refused to believe it. "You couldn't."

"Carin—"

"No, ma. Just stop." She couldn't understand why her mother had kept this from her. "Why would you do this? Why did you?"

"I wanted to protect you. I *needed* to protect you, to keep you near me."

"Protect me?" Liliana's face was hot. She took in another breath. Speaking louder now.

"To *protect* me? This was not yours to keep from me?" She sat now, unable to balance on her feet. "If you wanted to protect me, you would have told me." She placed a hand across her chest. Her wedding ring caught the light. "All these years…All these years… All these years." She rocked back and forth in the chair; her tears unceasing.

"Lili, I know. It was for the best, though." Amara took in a heavy breath. "It pained me to see you suffering all these years."

"Oh, I'm sorry for you, am. I can't imagine how hard it must have been watching, knowing you could help and never saying a word." Liliana's words were quick and punishing. Her ears felt hot to the touch. She looked away from her mother, shaking her head and tightening her lips.

"I kept them." Amara's voice quivered. "There were so many."

"Please, stop. I can't hear any more of this, Ma."

"No, I need to finish."

Liliana looked at her mother.

"Did Daddy know?"

Liliana leaned forward, but turned her face away from Amara, bringing her shoulder to ears in a wince. She held her breath waiting for her mother to answer.

"No, he didn't."

Liliana let out a breath and dropped her shoulders. She placed her hands in lap and looked at her mother.

"Where are the letters?"

She told her about the drawer in the kitchen. The drawer Liliana had walked past and even fingered as she stood in the kitchen waiting for water to boil. She'd never bothered to open it. She thought she knew where everything she could have needed was in that kitchen.

"Please, forgive me."

"What else can I do?" She took her mother's hand and squeezed, pushing all her hate and sadness. She left, closing the door, not looking back to meet her mother's eyes.

In the kitchen, she looked at Angela.

"You knew?"

She couldn't speak.

"Did you?"

"I…"

Liliana held up her hand, gesturing for Angela not to speak. She couldn't hear another word of betrayal. She opened the drawer. The drawer she had neglected, never knowing its contents could be so valuable.

"What is that?" Little Anna couldn't remain quiet a moment longer.

Liliana looked at Anna. She tried to smile, but the corners of her mouth were stuck.

She untied the red satin ribbon that fastened the letters.

"It's nothing." She wanted to believe this was true. She ran her fingers along the edges of the envelopes. The ink on some of the envelopes was smeared and faded, all written in his neat and measured script. Her cheeks were now wet with tears. She pressed them up to her face, hoping to smell him.

#

12 October 1954

My Dearest Liliana,

I think this is going to be my last letter. Your silence has been painful. Every waking moment since I got on that boat to get here has been for you. I know I wasn't the type of man your mother or father wanted you to marry. I did everything in power to make sure I could provide for you in the ways they could accept. No one could ever be good enough for you, Lili. You know that, right?

All these years I was struck that I hadn't heard from you. In my heart, I want to believe you just hadn't received any of my letters, but then I wonder how that might be possible. I know a lot of Gildonese moved to Canada. I heard from a few of our pisanos that your cousins on your father's side were in Montreal. Are you with them?

The other day I bumped into Gabriele Notti, and he told me he thought you were married. Is this true? When he told me this, my knees seemed to forget their purpose, and I nearly collapsed. Though I'm writing because I love you and want to hear back from you, I was also hoping you might break your silence and let me know.

If you did get married, I'd understand. So many nights I lay in bed imagining what it would be like to marry you. I could see the town marching behind you as walked toward the church. The dust from the road rising up like some sacred smoke. I would wait for you at the altar, my heart beat so wild, my hands shaking with excitement and fear. Would I be a good husband to you? Lord knows I would do anything to be everything you could ever want or need.

Gabriele didn't give me many details. He was just repeating something he'd heard from another pisano. You know news travels and changes. I keep holding out hope that it isn't true. If it is true, whomever this man is, I hope he makes you smile and laugh. I hope he holds your hand when you walk around the edge of town. I hope he steals kisses from you when no one is watching.

I hope he loves you with each waking moment and each sleeping breath.

Until I know for sure, I will wait for you. I'll keep checking my mailbox for a striped envelope from Italy with your name on the return address. I'll wait forever, Lili.

With all my love,
Raffaele

Part III: ANNA

Chapter 1

Anna's apartment was located near the Vatican. Painfully near. The walls were visible from her balcony. She stared at them on the mornings she sat outside sipping her espresso. The commanding walls reminded her that her chronic absence on Sundays had not gone unnoticed. She'd go this Sunday, if nothing came up, of course. This Sunday had come and gone for years. She had stopped going regularly when she moved out of her parents' house; stopped practicing. Because it took practice to be a Catholic. At least for Anna, it did.

When visiting her parents, she obliged and attended mass. Her mother would call her on Holy Days of Obligation. The phone would ring, and without a hello, her mother would begin, "Anna, don't forget tomorrow's Ash Wednesday."

"I know Ma. I don't have work tomorrow." Anna found the phone call unnecessary since the entire country was not working to accommodate the church. The priests did not get vacations from their obligations.

"Maybe you could go to confession, too. You know, start the Easter season clean." Anna hated when her mother did this. While she did think the ten years since her last confession had taken a toll on her mental health, Anna did not want to find the time to go. She was embarrassed. They would judge her. Her mother often explained to her the priests would not judge; they could not. They were there in place of God, only given the power to forgive her. She could never understand how the priest could just stand in for Christ and not judge. It seemed too simple. How could it be *that* easy to be forgiven? It felt like nonsense to her. It was likely the priests had heard much worse than what Anna had to confess. They had heard it all: murder, adultery, all of the Ten

Commandments broken and ignored. The Seven Deadly Sins committed all day, every day. Anna's confession would not offer them some intriguing surprise. So what she lived with her boyfriend? Who didn't these days? Living "in sin" was not something new for them. Even the phrasing was too much for her. "Living in sin" it was all too extreme. She wasn't attending mass regularly, neither was ninety percent of the Italian population. It was possible they would be relieved she was making an effort, though Anna was sure confession was for more of an active/practicing Catholic, versus a did-you-miss-me-it's-been-years type of Catholic.

She remembered as a child being annoyed by what her father called "*i Pasqualini*" and "*i Natalini.*" These were the people who remembered God twice a year. It would grain at her twelve-year-old mind. How could these people only come on Easter and Christmas? They took all the seats, talked during mass. It was distracting. Meanwhile, her family, while chronically late, was chronically there. Didn't they deserve to sit? Her mother was more understanding.

"Anna, at least they come. God is grateful for this."

"But what's the point of going if it's twice a year?"

"They're here, and that's enough." This was her mother's brilliant explanation for people who attended mass twice a year—never imagining her daughter would actually join the club. Or as the priest described them during the homily, "those who returned to God." What did that mean? Anna needed to know. Where had they gone?

"But…" Why was it enough for them, but not enough for their family?

"It's that simple. Now stop complaining." Her mother escorted Anna out of the church, "Did you do the sign of the cross?" Anna nodded.

"With the Holy Water?" Anna reached back into the basin, only letting her index finger nudge the water. She wouldn't dunk her hands deep into the water the way some of the others did. She didn't like it when her mother had dipped her little kid fingers into the water, forcing her to wet her whole face. She didn't want a wet forehead. She felt the same way about Ash Wednesday. For years, she strategically wore her hair in ways to cover the cross marked so clearly on her forehead. She also searched for reasons to wash it off; to remove the Catholic stamp. She finished the sign of the cross; in the name of the Father… There was no point in having this conversation again. For years, Anna and her mother had argued about this and the answer was always the same, "God is glad they're here." Anna wondered where her mother had gotten such insight. How could her mother have so much faith? Anna felt the Holy Water moisten her face. *I Pasqualini*'s and *Natalini*'s had won this time and would win every year after that.

Anna couldn't bring herself to tell her mother she had become the person she had criticized as a child. She felt a terrible weight at realizing she was a hypocrite. She feared bringing it up would result in some uncomfortable discussion with her mother, who would remember every word of that conversation from Easter twelve years ago. Her mother wasn't one to yell, instead, her eyes would get heavy and look away from Anna's as if carrying the weight of a sack of semolina. Anna also couldn't bear the shame of telling her mother she was living with Marco, her boyfriend. Telling her mother would make eye contact impossible between them for a few months, if not years. Her mother's disappointment would be like an open invitation for that elephant to fill silences during meals. Her mother's dark eyes would swell, her pupils would dilate—letting the disappointing news in. Her mother knowing would shatter the belief that like Liliana, she too had a raised a beautiful, well-behaved daughter. It would confuse Francesca. Her mother would question where had she gone wrong. Hadn't she been a good mother? Francesca would feel like a failure; although Anna, too, felt that Marco's moving in had been a line she never intended to cross. For months, Anna tried to analyze where this breach had started, what had let it happen. Her mother had often tried to show her that more times than not, it was more difficult to be good. Even when everyone else was wrong, the truth was the truth. Anna imagined trying to tell Francesca, and every version ended in her mother's collapse as she uttered, "I thought you were better than this, Anna. Better." Her eyes would close and everything would go black. Because of this, Anna had decided against it. When her parents would visit, she would ask Marco to stay at his mother's house and hide any evidence of his cohabitation with her

#

As they arrived at her apartment, she threw the pasta into the boiling water. She knew they had arrived because as the door opened, she heard her mother say, "*Permesso.*"

"*Entrata.*" They filed into the small kitchen and watched her as she finished preparing lunch.

She prepared a favorite childhood dish. Her Nonna Liliana had always made it for her when she visited Gildone. The eggplant and pasta worked well together when Anna took the time to prepare the eggplant properly. It was a two-day affair. Anna would watch her grandmother slice the eggplant into perfect circular slices, each slice the same width. After slicing the eggplant, her grandmother would salt the vegetable. It wasn't just a dash of salt. It was a blizzard of salt. Each slice received a generous coating.

"Nonna, that's a lot of salt. Isn't it too much?" Anna must have asked her this every time she watched her grandmother make the dish.

"No, Anna, the salt goes deep inside the eggplant so it isn't so mushy. You don't like it mushy, do you?" At the time, Anna didn't understand how the salt did this but trusted her grandmother nevertheless. There hadn't been a time Nonna Liliana had disappointed her in the kitchen. Nonna knew best.

After the salt storm, Nonna Liliana would take out every pot, pan, and dish she could reach. She'd layer the sliced eggplant into a large rectangular pan. Then she'd place a large pot filled with water directly on top of the eggplant. She would stack plates, pans, and pots creating a tower of kitchenware on top of the eggplant. It looked dangerous: the leaning tower of kitchenware.

"Nonna, aren't the dishes going to break?" Liliana always smiled when her concerned granddaughter asked about the dishes. She too had asked her Nonna Agostina about this.

"Don't you remember why we put the dishes on top of the eggplant?" Her grandmother tried to teach her granddaughter proper cooking techniques.

"Because of the salt?"

"Well, we do this so the water gets squeezed out."

Anna nodded. "So it's not mushy."

"*Essattamente.*" Anna smiled when her Nonna praised her culinary prowess.

It had taken several attempts and several failures for Anna to nearly perfect the dish. Her grandmother had "the hand" to make these dishes. That's what her Nonna called it "the hand." It sounded holy. Anna imagined her grandmother hands having mystical powers that could perfectly slice an eggplant, and how, on instinct, knew when to stop salting the vegetables. Anna knew it wasn't magic but learned. Still, her grandmother's cooking and baking, for that matter, was divine.

Anna learned the importance of slicing the eggplant evenly the first time she prepared the dish for her friends. She was rushing to slice the eggplant, not taking the time to make even circles. So, when Anna stacked her mother's antique plates, a housewarming gift, atop the eggplant, then placed the pots and pans on top of the plates, she understood why Nonna Liliana took the time to slice perfect circles and place them evenly in the rectangular pan. The pot filled with water crashed onto the counter spilling the water inside. Nonna sliced every eggplant the same way: She held the end of the eggplant steady and gently curved her fingers. Only her fingertips gripped the thick burgundy skin. As she sliced, her eyes scanned the circles. Her knife moved as if heated, and the eggplant butter. After several attempts, a puddle in the kitchen, and mushy eggplant, Anna never made the mistake again, deciding to make the dish only when she had set aside the right amount of time. There *was* something cathartic about the methodical and even slicing of the vegetable, the sound of only her knife gently nicking the cutting board. Anna never made it for her parents but thought having lunch in her apartment with Marco was a special enough occasion to make the nostalgic dish. Blending the past with the future was what the dinner table enabled.

If she intended on serving the eggplant dish, she would need to build the tower so it would do its work overnight. In the kitchen, standing on a stool, she retrieved the plates, removed the two eggplants from the refrigerator, and set up her station in a corner of the kitchen, making sure to tidy up as she went along. Anna was unable to function in a messy kitchen. Opened containers with spices, onion peels, minced garlic littered the countertop; she needed a clear space to be creative. She was unlike her mother and grandmother, whose kitchens resembled the

aftermath of a war zone. Liliana and Francesca watched Anna
cook, and both would look at each other saying, "I don't know
where she gets it from. I'm a mess in the kitchen." Her father
rarely made appearances in the kitchen as the chef, and when he
did cook dinner, he cooked up disasters.

There was one incident in particular that Anna always
remembered because it ended in a rare moment of family bonding.
While food brought them together, nothing really stopped
families from being pulled apart. Francesca rested after a long
hospital visit. Anna was six or seven and wanted only to make her
mother feel better.

"Babbo," she called out to her father, "can we make
mammina some lentil soup and roasted chicken?"

"I guess."

"Babbo," she continued to present her case. "It will make her
feel better. Mammina told me lentil soup has healing powers."
Francesca had also told her that eating broccoli would give her
the curliest hair in all of Italy. She believed this to be true until at
least eleven, and by then it was too late to stop eating broccoli
because she had grown to like it. She reached for his hand,
pushing aside his newspaper.

"Come, Babbo, I've already gotten it ready."

The two entered the kitchen. Anna had pulled out what she'd
thought were the right ingredients: the chicken, tomatoes, sugar,
lentils, carrots, and salad. Davide gently patted her head and went
to the phone. He called Liliana for a brief cooking lesson. Anna
watched as he carefully wrote the detailed instructions in his
immaculate handwriting.

"Okay, carina. Let's get started."

She was instructed to peel the potatoes, a chore she deplored.
Davide chopped the onions. He let the tears run down his face.

"Babbo."

"Sì, carina."

"You are crying because of the onions?"

"Yes, it's the onions."

They kept working, and the ingredients were prepped: the lemons were placed inside the chicken, the oven preheated, the carrots, potatoes, celery, and onions chopped. Anna was sure he had followed the instructions. He placed the soup ingredients in the pot and the chicken in the oven. The pot had no water, and he sautéed the vegetables, accidentally burning the onions. He then added too much water and not enough chicken stock. He dropped the bay leaves, and as he bent down to pick them up, the chicken caught fire in the oven. He opened the oven, pushing Anna away from the fire. He took baking soda and poured it over the chicken to help stop the fire from spreading.

"What is that smell?" Francesca asked as she entered the kitchen, holding her belly.

"We were making lentil soup and chicken," Anna explained.

"Well, trying to," Davide corrected.

Anna remembered the kitchen was a mess. There were lentils everywhere, onion skins on every counter, the lid to the containers were strewn across the kitchen, the dried oregano, basil, and garlic dusted the countertop. Her father left the oven door open, and the chicken let off soft gray plumes of smoke.

Her mother started to laugh, almost hysterically. Her father started to laugh as well, his eyes still watering. Anna was not sure why they were laughing and crying. Her mother got down on her knees, carefully, trying not to strain herself. Francesca then grabbed Anna, in an almost violent way and embraced her. It was as if her mother were making sure Anna was real, and since she was, she held on tight.

"Babbo, your cooking was too scary. Look, *mammina* is crying." Her parents exchanged looks, a private conversation. Her mother then left the kitchen and she and father cleaned up the mess, and instead of lentil soup and chicken, her father made Anna's least favorite dish, *ailio e olio.* It was the only thing her father could make without burning the kitchen down. It required two ingredients: garlic and olive oil. He fried the garlic in the olive oil and then dressed the pasta with it. As she grew older, Anna could rely on her father's *aglio e olio* after an attempt at any cooking. Her father didn't enjoy cooking the way she and her mother did. He also wasn't particularly skilled. Still, he would offer to help with dinner when her mother was unable. They could only tolerate so much *aglio e olio.*

Her grandmother, too, was always together, stable. When looking Liliana and Francesca, it wasn't always obvious that they were mother and daughter. Her mother didn't really look like a Farinacci. The Farinacci's had distinct almond-shaped eyes and skin that was almost golden after hours of sunlight. Francesca always favored her father's looked. She boasted dark, round eyes with thick lashes and an olive coloring. Francesca didn't even act like her grandmother, except sometimes in how she used her hands and cooked. In the kitchen, they were both a mess. Even though her grandmother's kitchen was always immaculate before and after meals, she, too, managed to get sauce everywhere. She wasn't sure if her grandfather had been neat and knew very little of her grandmother's past. She only knew that her grandfather had left before her mother was born. Liliana had removed any evidence that he even existed. Her grandmother's history was unclear to Anna. She hoped her mother and grandmother would share some of their past with her. She especially wanted to know more about her grandmother and grandfather. She wondered if he was a clean cook and how he managed under pressure. When Anna finished, it was as if she had never cooked in the first place. The only indication: a finished dish. She concluded that her cleanliness in the kitchen was a result of having to clean up after her mother's messes as a child.

While the eggplant sat underneath the pot, pan, and plate tower, she called her parents' house. The phone rang. Ring. Rang. Ring.

Her father answered, "*Pronto.*" Anna rolled her eyes, glad he couldn't see her. Her father was incapable of remembering events he had been told would occur. It had been a fault of his since he had become a father. Because of this, he left the remembering up to his wife. So, when Anna said, "I'll see you tomorrow, right, Papa?" his surprised response invited another eye roll.

"What? Tomorrow? No one told me about this."

But they had; Anna and her mother had been reminding him for two weeks.

"Papa, we told you."

"You and your mother are crazy. You didn't."

"We did—" She stopped herself, not about to argue.

"Anna, I would remember a trip to Rome." She debated backing herself up with evidence from her childhood. How many times had she told him she would be spending the day with a friend and he had looked at her stunned? Or when she would remind him of piano recitals and he would look at her and say, "You're still taking lessons?"

It wasn't that he couldn't remember, it was that he didn't bother to. He knew his wife and daughter would get him where he needed to be. It was the same with going to mass; he would work on the garden or schoolwork, always telling Francesca and Anna, "Call me when you're ready to go. I only need fifteen minutes." They would call him, and he would say, "okay, okay." Then, when he finally decided to get ready, they were all late. Anna wasn't sure why it didn't drive Francesca crazy. Her mother found his tardiness endearing.

"Whatever. Is Ma there? I want to remind her of the metro stop." She heard shuffling and mumbles of "no one told me" She heard him put the phone down.

"Francesca!" He shouted."FRAN-CHESSSSS-KAAAH!"

"What do you want?" she heard her mother say.

"What is the story with Rome?"

"Rome, what about it?" her mother replied. Her father still held onto the phone.

"We're going to Rome?"

"Yes, tomorrow. We told you." They continued back and forth.

"Hello," Anna said into the phone, hoping they could hear her.

"What is that?" Her mother asked.

"Hello?" Anna asked again.

"Oh, here. The phone is for you."

"Who is it?"

"Anna."

"Ciao, carina." Anna reminded her mother about the time, and the metro stop, stressing that they get off at the first Vatican stop, Cipro, not Ottaviano.

"So, it's not Ottaviano?"

"Exactly. Cipro."

"Didn't we get off on Ottaviano last time? It was definitely Ottaviano." Her mother's voice was confident.

"No," for the hundredth time, "you didn't. It's always been Cipro."

"Okay, carina. Cipro it is." Anna felt assured that she would not receive a call reminiscent of the "I don't see the pizzeria across the street" situation.

"Ciao," Anna released a deep breath.

"Ciao, ciao."

With the phone in hand, she stared into the kitchen, thinking about the rest of the menu; she'd prepare the rest tomorrow. Distracted, she heard the jingling of keys and walked over to the entrance to unlock the door. Marco stood, holding a loaf of bread, a bag from the market, keys, and his briefcase. Anna leaned forward, giving him a quick kiss.

"Can I put these down first?" he asked.

"Oh, I wasn't thinking." She took the bread, which was supported by his arm and sides, then kissed him again. "How was your day?"

"It was fine." He placed his briefcase by the door and walked towards the kitchen. "Eggplant?"

"Yes, remember—"

"Your parents are coming tomorrow…I know." He loosened his tie as he placed the milk, arugula, and marmalade into the fridge. After unloading the groceries, he walked toward the bedroom, undressing.

"I thought you were staying at your mother's house?" she asked.

"Again? You want to discuss this again?"

"No, I just want to make sure…" Her voice faded, embarrassed to have brought it up. Still, she would not back down. Having her parents over was enough. The visit entailed the food preparations, the mental preparations…the mental preparations. She had never had them over, and this time, Marco would be there. Her parents were well aware of his existence. They had spent holidays together, gone on trips together. Marco even spoke, on occasion, to Francesca on the phone, and because he answered, she kept him there; still, this was the first visit to her apartment in Rome. They had moved back to Campobasso after retiring. Anna worried there was too much evidence in her apartment indicating a co-ed environment. His history books dominated the bookshelf in the living room while her books were relegated to the office and bedroom. The bathroom also showed signs of Marco's presence, his electric shaver and man products renting the limited space on the counter. Although his products were minute compared to her shampoo, conditioner, shaving cream, body wash, face wash, and other products that had invaded the shower space, they were still there. Anna would scan the apartment for the third time that week in the morning, making sure his things were hidden. She had become so paranoid, she insisted he spend the night at his mother's house on the off chance that her parents arrived early, an occurrence as unlikely as the Pope knocking on her apartment door.

"It's just that—" she continued.

"I know," he said in his understanding teacher-voice, "they don't know we live together." He paused again. "It would be nice if you eventually informed them of our living situation since it has been a year."

"Maybe. I just think it would actually kill my mother," she said. "I've explained this to you."

"I'm just saying." He paused. "It would be nice."

She looked away from him, not knowing what else to say. He packed a duffle bag, putting his outfit for the parental lunch in his bag. She felt like a box of pasta after being shaken and broken, and she knew he hated seeing her like this. She couldn't blame him, either. She was impossible to handle, thinking irrationally about her mother dying as if in some melodrama. She wished he would shake her.

She just couldn't explain to him why their living situation was such an issue. Yes, part of it was that while society evolved, her mother held onto Catholic ideals that were out of fashion and ignored. Yet, Anna, too, struggled to understand why couples rushed to live together, but here she was doing the thing she didn't understand. It made Marco happy, and Anna enjoyed how their relationship imitated marriage, but that's what it was—imitation. Artificially flavored. They'd been together for years, were both settled in their careers, so why hadn't they at least gotten engaged? Anna wanted to be open with Marco, but when it came to marriage, she closed up, not wanting to put pressure on him. He reminded her often that they were happy. They were, but she wanted to believe it more thoroughly. Or was she? She'd never lived on her own. First, she lived with her parents, then she and a few of her girlfriends thought it might fun to live together, and now she was living with Marco. Each time she'd moved into a new place it hadn't been for herself. The only thing she had decided on in this apartment was where to put the bookcases.

"Well, aren't you going to stay for a while? I was thinking we could go for an *aperitivo*, then food with some of our friends. "She let him think about it. "After all, it is Friday."

He looked at her with a furrowed brow. He let out a breath through his nose, then rolled

his eyes. A slight smirk appeared in the corner of his lips. She pushed him onto the bed,

smiling.

"Let's go. Let's go. Let's go."

"Well, let me change."

He grabbed his duffle bag and briefcase on the way out to the bar and put it in his car. Rome was a city that people shouldn't drive in, but do regardless. Anna had told him to get rid of the car. It was a hassle, but he was independent "like the Americans" driving everywhere. They arrived at the bar, and slowly sipped an *appertivo*. The two were openly flirtatious with each other; to the outsiders watching them, it was not obvious that Anna's no-pressure-to-marry demeanor was actually tearing her up inside. As she drank, one glass after another, her mind wondered if his staying away for the night might force him to see how they practically were married. She noticed his body language was tense, even annoyed as they laughed with friends and complained about their students. Anna worried that her crazy paranoia would be what pushed him to end their relationship. She was relieved when his hand slid gently onto her thigh but retracted quickly as he reached for the bottle of wine and refilled his glass. She didn't know what to think. Marco dropped Anna off at their apartment, kissing her in a tempting way, trying to convince her to change her mind.

"Not tonight," she said, attempting to play hard to get, although she was already gotten. He huffed out a frustrated breath as she exited the car, towards the building.

"See you in the morning," he said, rolling his eyes as she stepped out of the car. He watched as the cobblestone gnawed at her heels. The stone did this to every woman in Rome. It was why Anna was convinced the shoe industry was so successful in Italy. She turned back and waved as she unlocked the gate, letting herself into the building.

#

Marco let himself into the apartment the next afternoon to see Anna having a meltdown in the kitchen. She was crouched in the corner, her knees to her chest, rocking back and forth. It was clear there had been a salad mishap.

"What is going on in here?" he asked.

"Oh, I'm fine." She didn't look fine and knew it.

"I don't think so. What's the problem?"

She stood up shaking a few leaves of lettuce out of her hair.

"Well," she began, "I was drying the salad with the damn salad spinner." She grabbed the empty salad spinner that had vomited salad all over the kitchen. "When the phone rang. I let go of the lid for one second, and then this—" She pointed to the floor, then the stove, then back to the floor. "—happened." She knew who was calling before looking at the caller ID.

"*Pronto*," she answered.

"Anna? Anna?" It was Francesca. Her voice sounded like it was in a tunnel. She was still in the subway.

"Mamma? Ciao? Mamma?"

"Anna, ciao. Okay, I can't hear you too well. We just got off at Termini, we should be there soon."

After hanging up with her mother, she began with vigilance preparing the rest of the meal. She still hadn't swept the apartment of Marco paraphernalia. Her hands were shaking and she was having a hard time calming her breath. Anna was embarrassed Marco had seen her like this, but it hadn't been the first time, nor would it be the last. She finished telling him about the morning. She could feel herself rambling.

"I don't know what I was thinking when I decided to use that salad spinner. Do you think we cleaned it all up?"

"I don't know, amore. We'll check again in a minute." He stood at the sink filling the pot with water. He salted the water and placed it on the stove. Anna heard the click of the gas igniting.

"Oh, they're going to be here any minute, and I forgot to get the fruit plate ready." As she blathered on and on, she noticed him walking towards her. "Marco, wh—" she began, but as he put his hands on her cheeks, she hushed.

"Please, breathe." He kissed her on the forehead. "It's going to be all right." He pulled her close. His chin resting on the top her head. His arms reached around her for an embrace. She felt the worry being sucked right of out her.

The water boiled, its lid banging against the pot; a prelude to the doorbell. Anna left the door unlocked, knowing they would eventually—inevitably—arrive.

"*Permesso.*" Her mother said this almost singing it.

"*Entrata.*" Her anxiety suddenly fueled her excitement.

Francesca's motherly instinct led her to the kitchen. She stood, watching her frantic daughter stirring the pasta.

"It smells just like when Nonna Liliana makes it," Francesca said, remembering so many days the two of them cooked together.

"It does not. Nonna makes it so much better." A smile swelled over Anna's face.

"I think I would know." Francesca grabbed the parmesan on the table and began to grate it over the pasta.

"We're late because she only gives me a five-minute warning...." Anna heard her father discussing his keen instincts with Marco in the living room. Anna looked at her mother, and the two of them rolled their eyes together.

"I gave you more than five minutes. You're always late. Ever since I met you," Francesca interrupted.

Davide turned to Marco, pointing at Francesca, who stood between the kitchen and the living room.

"I'm only late because I have to wait for you." Do you hear this?"

Marco nodded and looked as if he wasn't sure what to say next.

"Leave him out of this, Babbo," Anna called from the kitchen, straining the pasta, her face towards the living room, but away from the steam. "Does anyone want something to drink? An *aperitivo* before we eat?"

Everyone declined. Anna shrugged her shoulders and continued with the lunch preparations. Marco and Davide sat talking. It was mostly her father who did the talking, reminiscing with Marco about his days as a teacher and student. Her father had a way with remembering the days when he was a student, forgetting he had worked with students daily for over thirty years. He spoke as if the students he taught were no comparison to how students were when he was a kid, convinced his classroom was filled with no-good, lazy students. The one and only Thomas Gradgrind sat in Anna's living room. The conversation moved its way to the dining room table that Marco and Anna had moved onto the balcony.

"I'm telling you, we couldn't get away with anything," her father continued. "Anything!" Marco looked to Anna for help.

"Babbo, when you retire, are we still going to have to hear these stories?"

"Probably," Francesca muttered. She had heard them so many times, she had begun to incorporate them into her own childhood memories.

"I think even Marco has them memorized." Anna winked at him as she placed the crushed chili peppers on the table between her and her father's place. They were the only two in the family that needed extra heat in their food.

Even though there were only four of them, they managed to make as much noise as a classroom full of students, each raising their voice as the decibel level rose. Her father was almost shouting his story to Marco and they sat right next to each other. Francesca and Anna spoke loud trying to hear each other over the men.

The summer weather commenced complementing the menu Anna had designed. The *pasta e melanzana* was a light dish. She then served a refreshing salad of cucumbers and tomatoes dressed in olive oil, oregano, pepper, and salt. For dessert, she served a fruit tart. She had cheated and purchased the dessert from the bakery down the street. Her grandmother would have been disappointed.

"I'm sorry I didn't have time to bake this myself, it's been crazy with Easter and summer being around the corner."

"It would only be a problem if Nonna was here," Davide pointed out.

"Speaking of Nonna, when is the last time you called your grandmother?" Francesca asked.

"Not sure. It's been a while." Anna was ashamed. She was terrible at keeping in touch with her Nonna.

"Well, she was telling me the other day, and I hate to say this, but she sounded very depressed, she would love to have you visit."

Anna looked at Marco. She didn't want to spend days in Gildone alone, just she and her grandmother. Gildone had three establishments still in business, the butcher shop, Nonna's bakery, and the bar. Surely she wasn't expected to visit for more than an afternoon, a day at most.

"She sounded depressed?"

"Yes, she wasn't herself." Francesca's voice faded. She looked over the balcony. Her eyes rested on the Vatican walls.

"Ma? What's going on?"

"I just think you should go see your grandmother. She needs you." She continued, "You know she's all alone in that house. She probably needs to be around your young energy."

"I guess. It has been a while." Anna hadn't spent time with her grandmother in years. She saw Liliana on holidays when she picked her up at the train station near her parents' house. A weekend visit, with summer having arrived, wouldn't be too terrible. There wasn't much to do in Gildone, which meant she'd have a chance to catch up on some reading. And since she and Marco had moved in together, they were spending all of their time together. Visiting her grandmother would give Marco the opportunity to miss her. This would be as good for grandmother as for her and Marco.

"You'll call her then?"

"Yeah, I'll work something out."

She considered asking Marco to join her but decided against it. There wasn't much to do in Gildone, and the town was quite awkward around strangers. She imagined them whispering to each other about who that man was, why was he here with Liliana's granddaughter, they weren't even married. She recalled a summer spent there a few years back when down the street from her grandmother's house. Two American girls were visiting their aunt. They had been sent to buy bread at the bakery, and when they passed the center of town, the men and women stared at them, and then back at each other, whispering about who they were. Couldn't they have gone to the other bakery closer to their aunt's house? Anna wondered why they were so concerned about where these strangers bought their bread, especially since they were buying from her grandmother's bakery, a place they had sworn allegiance to when the other bakery opened years before Anna's mother had even been born. No, bringing Marco was not a good idea. Anna was in no mood for the Gildonese dramatics.

"Good." Francesca said this as if closing the lid on a jar of sticky marmalade, sealing its contents so easily spilled. Anna knew there was no way to avoid visiting her grandmother, and the more she thought about this, she decided it wouldn't be so bad getting out of Rome, breathing the untainted Gildonese air. Also, Anna recalled having spent many lovely summers with Liliana and Aunt Angela in Gildone. She remembered the church festivals and thought it really had been too long since she'd been to one. There was lots of dancing and old world culture for her to absorb. Not to mention, it was clear by her mother's tone that it had been decided for her.

After the table had been cleared and the dishes washed, Anna walked her parents to the metro stop. She enjoyed walking after a large meal. They walked along the Vatican walls. Francesca looked up at their commanding presence, wishing she had lived in Rome as a young girl, enjoying the Catholic ambiance. They walked towards the metro station and stopped to let a group of nuns cross. Anna had escorted them to the subway as an excuse to take a walk, but also because she worried that as the sun set, they would get lost. Unfamiliar places tended to change in appearance at different times of day.

Chapter 2

The phone continued to ring. Liliana was either at the bakery or downstairs smoking. Anna tried once more, and when no one answered, she called the bakery. Her grandmother had the line installed only because Francesca had insisted she be reachable. The request for the phone line had taken three years of mother-daughter bickering to pass. Liliana, who had become so set in her ways, was often too stubborn to handle. Though the line had been activated for nearly six years, Liliana answered only when she felt like it, rarely. The bakery line rang and rang and just as Anna decided to give up, thinking it must be some kind of sign—

"*Pronto.*"

"Nonna?"

"Carina, how are you? You must have remembered you had a grandmother today. Even my own daughter forgets she has a mother. It must be the Roman air."

"I didn't forget about you. I've been busy. How is everything? Mamma said you weren't feeling well."

"Francesca is crazy. I'm fine."

"She said you didn't sound fine. Are you sure everything is okay?"

"Yes." Anna could tell she was lying; her grandmother coughed then cleared her throat.

"Well, that's good. I'm glad to hear you're doing well."

"I can't talk long, carina. I just put some bread in the oven."

"Oh, well I was really calling because my summer break is coming up, and I was thinking I would come down and stay with you for a while. I need a break from Rome."

"Well, you know you're always welcome here. You know what we could do when you come here?"

"What?"

"I was thinking I should show you how to bake. I know your mother neglected to show you how."

"I would love that."

The last summer Anna had spent in Gildone, she was fourteen. She had promised her grandmother she would learn to bake that summer, but a cute boy from a neighboring town had distracted her from her grandmother's lessons. She never heard the end of it from her grandmother, who wanted to teach her how to make millefoglie, but more importantly, sfogiatelle. It was a recipe that had been passed on since before Senore Farinacci's father had taken over the bakery. Someone had to learn it, and it wouldn't be Francesca. She was a klutz and a mess when she baked, neglecting the constant reminder to be precise. Whenever they spoke, her grandmother repeatedly told Anna she was worried the sfogiatelle recipe would die with her. Anna was the last chance.

"Okay, so you call me when you're on your way."

#

That evening after she and Marco cleaned the kitchen, they sat outside on the veranda. The Vatican walls lit up as the sun began to set. The air began to cool. Marco brought a bottle of wine and two glasses outside and placed it on the patio table between them.

"Thank you for helping me earlier, by the way."

"Of course." He turned to smile at her. "What was I supposed to do let you spiral?"

"I know. I get a little crazy when it comes to my parents."

"A *little* crazy?" He rolled his eyes. "You were shouting into the phone, Anna. I'm surprised the police didn't show up.

Anna knew better than to call her mother after talking to her grandmother, but she wanted to let her know she'd spoken with Liliana and was giving her the dates she'd be in Gildone. This devolved into a lecture on etiquette, among other things.

"I just—"

"I know."

"It just drives me crazy because she was going on and on about how I *had* to go visit Zio Gianni. As if I was going to go Gildone where there is nothing to do and *not* see family. That place is so small, chances are I'll see them when I get off the bus.

"Anna, your hands are shaking."

"Ah, I don't know why I care so much about what they think. But between my mother and her constant nagging about Zio Gianni and asking about how things are going with— "she stopped herself. She was too tired to talk about the status of their relationship…again. It just seemed like everyone she knew was getting married, and the longer they stayed together without getting engaged, the harder it was for her to be around him. She and Marco had been together for a

"Anyway, I called my grandmother today."

"Yeah?"

"It's been a long time since I saw her, and my mom made it sound like things aren't good."

Anna noticed Marco looking out at the street.

"It will be nice to spend some time with her. She gets lonely, though she'd never admit it." Anna remembered how the last summer she was there she tried to sneak down early one morning to make the two of them espresso, she found Nonna Liliana sitting at the kitchen table staring at a stack of letters. Her grandmother's handkerchief rest next to the letters, wrinkled and used. Anna never asked about them.

"Mmmhmmm." He wasn't listening.

"Who knows maybe I'll finally learn to bake." She laughed and looked out at the tile rooftops. "I'll probably stay through the festival then come back up here in time for work to start up again."

"That's a long time." He took a big gulp of wine.

"I guess. It will be good for my Nonna, though."

Anna wasn't sure what to make of Marco's moderate indifference. She wiped a drop of condensation from the wine glass. She placed the glass to her lips and took a small sip.

#

The last two months of the school year were always the toughest. The students only thought of summer after Easter passed, and the same was true for the teachers. They were eager for their almost three-month vacation. The air was no longer fresh and inviting, it was humid and hot, forcing the students to slow down. Back at the apartment, she and Marco had started to fight continuously. Anna wanted to know where they were going. Was he ever going to propose?

"I will ask you when I'm ready."

"It's been almost six years. Either you love me or you don't."

"I love you, you know that."

"Do I?"

"Don't you?"

"I don't know." She sat down on their bed, her hands covering her face.

"If you don't know that I love you, you have to understand there is a bigger issue here. Anna, I can't take the pressure."

"I know. It's just...where is this going?"

The longer a couple stayed a couple, the more they became one and stopped being two separate people. Everything they did was wrapped up in each other. They saw friends together. Walked to work together. Made big decisions together. After six years of together, Anna was starting to forget what she was like before him. They met at the tail end of university. This was usually the time when people started to figure out who they were as individuals, but she and Marco did that...together. She didn't have to look in the mirror to realize that she couldn't recognize her face. She knew herself only when she cooked. That was what she loved. She loved the rhythm of her knife meeting the cutting board, and the sound of onions hitting hot oil and hissing. She loved running her fingers over freshly picked tomatoes and sticking her hands into a fresh salad, oil, herbs, and salt covering each lettuce leaf and sliced cucumber. She didn't love teaching, she didn't love reading. The only thing she loved was the food.

"Aren't we happy?" he said. "I'm happy, you seem happy. I don't know what to tell you."

"I think one of us needs to move out. I feel..." She didn't want to say "suffocated," but that's what she felt. She felt that the constant reminder of how unofficial their situation was cutting off her breath.

His eyes widened as she spoke. He ran his hands through his hair and nodded.

"Where is this coming from?" He walked over to her and sat down next to her. Marco put his arm around her. She pulled away from him.

"I think this upcoming trip to my grandmother's will be good." She didn't know what else to say.

"I was thinking the same thing." He looked away from her.

"Marco, I'm just so confused. I know I don't want to stop seeing you. I just think we need to live apart."

"I need you, Anna." Did he not need her enough to be his wife?

She looked at him then back down at her hands. They sat next to each other in silence. The sound of traffic and people talking on the street filled the room. All Anna could think about was how she couldn't go back in time and change this now. Had she made a mistake? She looked down at her hands again. She ran her fingers from her left hand over the ring finger of her right. Quiet tears fell down her face.

"So, what do we do now?" She wanted to say it over and over again. She looked over at him. He placed his hand on her shoulder and rubbed her back. She leaned into him. He stood up.

"I think I'm going to stay with my parents."

"Okay." Anna reached for him then pulled back. She pursed her lips. "That's probably a good idea."

"I'll get my things during the week."

She put her hand on the bed where Marco was sitting moments ago. Her chest felt as if it had been filled with hot metal and the heat was painfully radiating out of her.

"You'll still have dinner here, right?" He looked at her with an incredulous glare. She averted his eyes and let the tears fall, wetting the collar of her shirt.

"Let me think about it."

He grabbed some of his things and placed them in a suitcase by the door.

"Are we going to be okay?" She needed to know.

"I hope so." He kissed her on the forehead, then turned his back to her to leave.

#

The first few weeks of their separation, Anna struggled to sleep in the bed alone. She cried most nights. With summer vacation looming, she was mostly distracted at work. At work, she would start to draft him a quick email asking him about dinner then stare at the screen. She'd shake her head, trying to clear her thoughts. When she walked in the door, she was reminded of Marco's absence once again, hanging her keys by the door only to find his hook empty. In the morning, she prepared entirely too much espresso, not drink it all, and pour it down the sink: an all too poignant metaphor. What a waste. Six years. 2, 109 days down the drain with the espresso. But who was counting?

He didn't turn up for dinner. Instead, he came with boxes and a suitcase. She had stopped insisting he stay, not wanting to be a nag or pathetic. And with only a few weeks until she was going to leave for Gildone, their separation was starting to look permanent.

"Just so you know, I'm going to Gildone in a few weeks," she told him as he packed up his movies and some books.

"I know. Are you still planning on staying with your Nonna Liliana?"

"Yep." She shuffled some mail in her hands. "I haven't really gotten to talk to you about it, but there has been a lot going on with her."

"Like what?"

"Well, my mother called me earlier in the week to tell me that my grandfather, Domenico, has been trying to sell the house because he needs the money to pay off his gambling debts and medical bills."

"How can he sell the house?"

"Apparently, because my grandmother is still legally married to him, he has ownership of the house."

He said nothing. It infuriated Anna that her grandfather was hurting her grandmother from so far away. That house had been in their family for centuries. It was on Farinacci Street. They had lived there for so long the townspeople decided to rename the streets.

"She needs me."

"Sounds like it."

"You know, the festival of Santa Monica starts at the end of July. You should come."

"We'll see." He returned to his packing. "What are you cooking tonight?"

"*Carbonara.*"

"My favorite. Throw some extra pasta for me."

Chapter 3

She got off the bus in Gildone, a small suitcase in hand. The same bench inhabited by the town's old men still rested under the large elm tree. Gildone always looked the same to Anna, and in the summer, the humid air smelled sweet and dusty all at once. It was early afternoon, so she headed first to drop off her suitcase. She passed Angela's house and popped in for a quick hello.

"Oh, Liliana will be so happy to see you. I haven't seen her so depressed in years. Since the whole le—it's been a long time."

"Really? She said she was fine when I called her, but I could tell she wasn't herself."

"It must get to her, being all alone. She barely eats with us, only on Sundays, really. She bakes, goes to mass, and sleeps."

"That's so sad, Zia."

"I know. Did your mother tell you about the house?"

"Yes, I can't believe it."

"I know. What a—" She put her hand to her mouth biting her bent index finger. "This has been going on for years, and she's just now telling us. He wrote Liliana a year ago, asking her for a divorce again. She, of course, refused. Sometimes she…. anyway, he threatened to sue her if she didn't."

"How is she handling it?"

"She's getting old. She smokes. She thinks I don't know that she smokes, but her front yard reeks of it. If she dies before him, the property belongs to him. All so that she could make a point."

"What's she going to do?"

"I keep telling her to sign the papers. She won't. This has been going on for so long." She shook her head. "Your mother didn't tell you this?"

"I guess she didn't want me to worry."

"You know, when your grandfather left, Liliana was never the same. Then he asked her for a divorce. Your mother was in high school the first time he asked her; it nearly killed her. Every time she gets the mail, it's another story. It's too bad she won't go live with your mother, but she'd never leave Gildone. Still, she shouldn't be alone. It's too much for her."

Hearing this upset Anna. Her grandmother didn't have to live alone. Her mother had offered hundreds of times to have her stay with her and Davide. Her excuse was its close proximity to Campobasso and how chaotic it was there. "All the traffic. All those people. No thank you," she would say each time Francesca offered. Perhaps she could change her grandmother's mind, or at least lift her spirits.

Before heading to the bakery, she decided to drop her bag off. On the way back from her grandmother's house, she passed the church and what used to be the dress shop. Her cousins had moved it to Campobasso and business took off. They were so busy that they, too, rarely made it to Gildone. Anna took in the center of the village. There were only two indications there was still any life left in Gildone: the men sitting at the bar in the middle of the day not working, and the satellite dishes bolted to almost every balcony.

She opened the bakery door and remembered why, as a child, she always begged her mother to let her stay one more week for summer. The antique cash register her grandmother didn't use, the racks of pastries from which she had tried every one, and the big back room with the floured table where she so often watched her grandmother make sfogiatelle was all she needed to be content. She breathed it in: the smell of sugar and yeast. This place had a history, a history she didn't know.

"Ciao, Nonna!"

"Carina." Liliana waddled toward her granddaughter. "Did you say hi to Angela?"

"Yep."

"Good, we don't want her to get offended." She motioned for Anna to follow her to the back. She pulled chairs out for the two of them, and they gabbed about what was new and how it had been too long. When it was time to close, they grabbed their purses and began walking up the hill towards the house.

"Carina, I'm so tired. I just want to close this place down," she admitted.

"Well, why don't you? You don't need to keep it open. The other bakery could handle the bread and pastries for this small town, though yours are the best. Ever."

"Aeeee! Can you imagine what people would say if Liliana Farinacci closed up the bakery?"

Anna didn't know how to argue with her grandmother's logic that was grounded in excuses and the opinions of others. The front yard was a mess, not at all how Anna remembered. Liliana unlocked the door, and it was then Anna noticed all the filth. When she dropped her bag off earlier, she hadn't noticed the spider webs and dust that coated the living room that was no longer lived in, and the piles and piles of dishes by the sink. Angela hadn't mentioned it. The house had been like this for years; it was obvious by the atrophy. How could the woman who had forced Francesca to freak over a drop of sauce on the stove live here?

"Well, Nonna, what should I prepare for supper?"

"You prepare? No, go upstairs, change out of those clothes. I'll take care of supper."

She knew there was no point in arguing. Grandmothers lived days longer knowing they could prepare a meal for their grandchildren. She walked up the dusty stairs, past what was supposed to be her grandmother's bedroom. She hadn't slept there in years; the room was untouched. The stairs were too much for her. In the formal living room, a hutch with dusty knick-knacks stood awkwardly. She looked out the window and noticed her grandmother's garden full of weeds and was totally overgrown. Everywhere she looked she saw a mess. This place needed love.

#

"Ma, you should see it. It's disgusting. I barely slept last night knowing how badly it needed to be cleaned."

"Well, that's why you're there. You have to help her."

"I know, but I think the house is too much for her. She doesn't sleep upstairs. I'm worried about her."

"I know. I am too, but what can we do? She's so stubborn."

"Yeah." She took in a breath. "Well, Ma, I better get going. We'll talk soon. Ciao."

Anna closed the phone line and looked around her. Her grandmother now slept in the guest room downstairs, which was close to the bathroom and the kitchen. She had a small television on the kitchen counter that was dwarfed by all the dishes. Anna looked for the cleaning supplies and found them under the kitchen sink.

"Nonna, I'm going to bring you lunch and then come back here. I have a few things to take care of. I promise we will bake tomorrow."

"Yeah, yeah," Liliana responded. Anna could see her grandmother was disappointed, but something had to be done about the house. The previous night at dinner, Liliana eagerly explained to Anna how she'd begun to experiment with ingredients and hoped Anna could provide some new ideas for flavor combinations. Her grandmother mumbled something about prayers and stood up. Liliana left, leaving Anna to begin the cleanup. She decided to clean the kitchen first, then she'd head to the bakery in the afternoon.

Anna entered the bakery with a panini for her grandmother. She had laced the bread with olive oil and oregano and added fresh prosciutto, arugula, and buffalo mozzarella. Her hair was pulled back, and her oval face coated with dust.

"What have you been up to?"

"Nothing."

"Anna?"

"You'll see. Don't worry about it."

She cleaned the cabinets, making sure every item had a place and threw out junky old Tupperware and knickknacks that only took up space. She labeled containers for sugar, flour, semolina, corn-flour, and all the other loose ingredients. She threw out the awkwardly shaped containers her grandmother kept. She scrubbed the floors on her knees, making sure to get all the corners, removing dust from the moldings. She prepared her grandmother's room, folding and placing all her clothes in neat piles. When she finished, she showered and finished folding the last of the laundry. She returned from the bakery early, and as the sun began to set, she put a pot of water to boil and sautéed eggplants in olive oil and garlic.

"What happened here? Why are there so many bags of garbage out front?" Liliana said as she entered the kitchen. She stopped. "You did this?"

"I had to."

"You're just like your mother and your great-grandmother."

"I know. Are you happy?"

"I've wanted to do it for years, I just couldn't….I couldn't do it." She breathed in the dust-free air. "I am too tired."

She sat down at the already set table and openly thanked God for an energetic granddaughter. Anna inhaled the smell of the eggplants, wine, and garlic.

"It smells almost as good as when I make it." A smile freed her face from the wrinkles.

"I can't make it like you, Nonna."

#

The summer moved slowly. Each day Anna cleaned, threw out clutter, and organized another room. Her grandmother's old bedroom was the last room she undertook. It rested in the corner of the house and was the only room with a balcony. Since the house was built on a hill, the room had a view of the valley below. Anna could see the winding road and the technicolor farmland. There was no closet, only an armoire with old clothes. Anna emptied the drawers, vacuumed, and dusted. She returned everything to its place. One of the nightstands had a heavy gray stone ashtray. On the other side, the drawer contained a box with a red satin ribbon poking out from its lid.

Anna opened the box and saw old letters. She'd seen this stack of letters before. It was her last summer. This must of have been the letters she'd seen her grandmother with that morning. Anna flipped through the letters. The handwriting on all of them indicated they were from the same person. She noticed the letters were all postmarked from Venezuela. Were these from her grandfather? How strange. She remembered her mother and aunt told her how her grandfather Domenico had never written.

She looked at the stamps from the post office: 1950. These were from before her mother was born. She put the box down and went to the phone.

"Pronto," Francesca answered.

"Hey, Ma. Really quick. When was Nonna Liliana married?"

"1953. Why?"

"Oh, I was just curious." She hadn't thought through how this conversation would go.

"Is that all? I'm in the middle of a rosary, carina."

"Yes. That's it." For once, she was relieved that her mother was always praying.

"Okay. Ciao."

"Thanks, Ma. Ciao." She hung up the phone more confused than before. Who would have written to Nonna in 1950?

When she entered the room and saw the stack of letters on the bed, Anna found the temptation to read them was unrelenting. If Liliana had wanted her to know about them, she would have told her. If Anna knew what was in the letters maybe she could help her grandmother. She stood at the foot of the bed staring at the letters. Anna heard the ticking of the clock next to her grandmother's bed. Nonna Liliana would be back in a few hours. She needed to finish dusting and mopping.

As she picked up the letters to return to them to the box, a few fell to the floor. The paper was almost sheer. The writing small and deliberate. Anna held one of the letters that unfolded as it fell with one hand and placed the rest of the stack on the bed.

17 February 1954

My Dearest Liliana,

I couldn't help but think to write to you on this perfect, sunny day. The sun is shining in the center of the sky, and there isn't a cloud in sight.

What I wouldn't give---

Anna looked up from the letter. She shook her head as if trying to forget what she had just read. What was she doing? She looked at the stack of letters and placed the few that had fallen with the rest and secured them with the red satin ribbon. She closed the box, not wanting to be more of a snoop and replaced them in the nightstand. Once the house was cleaned, she opened all the windows and doors and cleared the air.

#

A few weeks had passed since she'd started cleaning, and Anna had learned to make the pizza minestra and polenta almost as perfect as Liliana's. She noticed that with each clean room, her grandmother appeared to be more like herself. Her grandmother was eager to work in the kitchen and not as lethargic. there was more buoyancy in her spirit. Anna hoped that the small change would be the fresh start she needed.

At the bakery, Liliana first showed Anna how to make millefoglie. It looked difficult because the dough had so many layers thanks to all the butter. The real the trick was in the thick creamy custard that held it all together.

"Carina, you need to really watch the filling." Liliana stood next to Anna as she whipped the filling by hand. At first, Anna's arms grew tired from the whipping motion. She woke with soreness in her shoulders and biceps.

"Like this?" Anna asked as she took a small spoon of the millefoglie filling and handed to her grandmother.

"That's good, but it's still too soft."

Anna learned quickly. She absorbed the details and nuances. It only took her two weeks to pick up the filling for the millefoglie. The dough would take a little bit longer.

"To make the dough, first we need to dissolve the salt in a small bit of water." Her nonna was such a good teacher. She was patient and forced Anna to think about the purpose of the next steps.

"Nonna, you're like a chemistry teacher."

"Get out of here. I just play with flour all day." She slapped Anna's hands.

"Don't forget to dust the table with flour after you add the water." Her grandmother warned. Anna watched her grandmother then repeated the same step with her ingredients. "Once the salt is dissolved into the water, we add it to the flour." Her grandmother placed a few grams of flour on the table in a mound. She took Anna's hand and created a small crater for the water. The two worked the water into the flour.

"Am I doing this right?" Anna's hands were sticky from the dough.

"Keep going until it's not sticky anymore." Her grandmother added more flour to the mixture. "It was looking a little too wet."

Anna watched as grandmother made a batch of dough next to Anna. The two worked side by side in the heat of the bakery with the ovens blasting fire while they baked bread, and cookies, and pastries. Anna imagined her grandmother as a gatekeeper, only letting privileged guests past her.

Chapter 4

After a morning of cleaning and lunch, Anna prepared her grandmother an espresso, then the two were to walk to the bakery together for Anna's baking lesson. The sfogiatelle were taking longer to learn than Anna had anticipated. Her natural talent was not enough. They were too difficult to shape. She was too rough, always tearing the dough, just like her mother when she tried to learn years ago. On this morning, Liliana left earlier to get the bread and other pastries ready for the day. She was running behind because Francesca had called, talking Anna's ear off about the house and Venezuela and her stubborn mother.

"Have you talked to your grandmother about the house?" Her mother asked. Francesca would always call after 9, knowing her mother was already at the bakery.

"No, Ma. I'm waiting for her to bring it up."

"Ha! Well, good luck with that."

"Okay, Ma. Nonna is waiting for me"

"All right, carina. Ciao."

"Ciao." Anna hung up the phone then locked the house doors fifteen minutes after her grandmother left.

She had just reached the center and was about to turn towards the bakery when she stopped by an older gentleman. His posture was upright, and he had a full head of white hair. His eyes were deep set and pensive. He squinted his eyes as if trying to decipher the meaning of a complicated poem.

"Excuse me."

"Yes."

"Do you know who Liliana Farinacci is?"

Anna stopped to turn and face the man.

"Yes. Why?" Anna wondered if he was an uncle from a neighboring town or maybe some government official looking to discuss the house with her grandmother. He couldn't have been from the village since everyone knew everyone in Gildone. He was tall for a man his age. Anna could see he had once been a strong young man and very handsome. He cocked his head to the side as he looked at Anna and smiled like he was keeping a secret. She returned the smile only to see him straighten up and look at the bench under the elm tree. A flicker of sadness moved across his face as his smile vanished. He appeared rapt in his memories. He was well-dressed, compared to many of the men in town. His clothing was very precise. He looked as though he were a man who was built for labor, but chose to work behind a counter instead.

"I knew you would know her. You look just like she did when I met her."

"My family has been telling me that for years. She's my grandmother. How do you know her?"

"I'm Raffaele, a very old friend of Liliana's."

"Raffaele? I've never heard of you."

"Oh no? We were always together, the two of us, since were kids. Do you know where I can find her?"

"She's at the bakery. I'm headed there." He stepped away from Anna. "I'll walk with you if you'd like."

"Well…"

Anna watched him as he decided.

"I'm sure she'd be happy to see you."

"No, maybe another time." He paused. "Will you tell her I said hello and that I'm back?"

"I can do that. Any other messages?" She wanted to know more about him and Liliana.

"Tell her I'm staying with my nephew Vincenzo Pasquarella."

"Will do."

"Ciao."

"Ciao"

"Ciao."

He walked away from her in a hurry. He was an adorable old man. She wondered how he'd known Liliana. She knew very little about her grandmother's past, and what she did know was learned second-hand from her mother. Raffaele, she repeated his name, trying not to forget, Raffaele. She walked away from him smiling.

She entered the bakery to see there was a long line of customers. She helped her grandmother take care of them and her recent conversation slipped away from her as she interacted with the customers. When the bakery was empty, she and her grandmother continued their lessons.

"Carina, are you ready to try making these again?"

"Not really. I'm so terrible at it."

"You'll get it."

All day she and her grandmother worked on the sfogiatelle. Anna was frustrated. Even after almost a month of practicing with the sfogiatelle dough, she still was terrible at it. Liliana continued to mention the improvements she noticed. Anna finally used enough flour to control the cones of dough. She also filled them with the appropriate amount of filling. The one hiccup she had was with the shaping of the shell. Liliana, too, struggled with them. She explained to Anna how her father would make her practice every day. Hour after hour until she learned to shape the outer edges carefully, pushing layer after layer of fine dough into its shell shape. Anna watched Liliana as she shaped the sfogiatelle. She did it without thinking. Her hands knew precisely what to do. She made one after the other so fast, filling each one as she went along. Each shell with perfect symmetrical layers that, after being baked, would be crisp and sprinkled with sugar.

#

The two were sitting in the kitchen enjoying a post-dinner espresso, a summer indulgence Anna decided she would adopt when she returned to Rome.

"I almost forgot to tell you, Nonna."

"What?"

"The other day, on my way to the bakery, this man bumped into me. He asked me to tell you hello."

"Oh yeah? Who?"

"He said his name was Raffaele."

Liliana's hands seemed to forget she was holding a cup. Her espresso cup dropped to the ground, shattering. Pieces of porcelain and drops of espresso scattered onto the ground. Anna looked at her grandmother who was unable to speak or breath, incredulous. Anna could see her grandmother holding her breath. Anna needed to know who he was. Raffaele, she said to herself, Raffaele.

"Nonna?"

Liliana looked up at Anna. Her facial expression was confused as if Anna's voice were muffled. She fell from her chair. Anna pushed the shattered cup pieces away from her grandmother.

Anna stared at her, trying not to panic. She tried to wake her but couldn't. She called Angela, who rushed over.

"What happened?" She took a damp cloth to her sister's face.

"I was telling her how I bumped into a man in the center the other day. He asked me to tell her hello. Said his name was Raffaele."

Angela stopped. She looked down at her sister, who was starting to come to.

"Did you just say Raffaele?" Angela asked.

"Yes, Raffaele. Who the hell is he?"

"I don't believe it. I just don't believe it."

"Believe what?"

"After all these years..."

"What? After all these years, what? Please, someone, tell me."

Liliana stood up with the help of Anna and Angela who escorted her to her room. Anna brought her tea and rested a blanket over her comforter.

"Are you okay?"

"I'm fine."

Anna was confused. Who was this man? She couldn't tell if this was an occasion to be happy, or angry, or thrilled, or relieved, or afraid.

"I'm fine," she repeated.

"Good. Rest up, because tomorrow I have a lot of questions."

#

The following morning, Anna woke to find her grandmother sitting at the kitchen table, staring at the stack of old letters. The same red satin ribbon rest on the table next to them.

"This is Raffaele."

"What?" Her grandmother pushed the letters toward Anna and watched her granddaughter as she read, sipping her espresso.

#

"She waited until she was half-dead to tell me he had actually written," Liliana explained. "I can't do anything now. I'm almost eighty. My life's been wasted."

"What are you talking about, wasted?" Anna asked. "You don't even know why he's here." Anna looked at her grandmother. Liliana held the red ribbon in her hands. She looked down at the letters. She reached across the table for her cigarettes.

"Does it matter why he's here?" Liliana inhaled the smoke. "All I know is that once word gets out that he's here, the talking will start all over again."

Anna wasn't sure what her grandmother meant by this since she had moved away before experiencing the village gossip, but her mother had told her it could be unrelenting. Still, would the town really care about an old woman and her former sweetheart?

"How did you meet Raffaele?"

"We were always together, even as kids."

"He told me that."

"You know, I hated him at first. But then, when he started to work and we didn't spend our days together, I realized how much I actually loved him."

Anna could see her grandmother's pain and happiness. How could her Nonna Amara have done such a thing?

"You know, carina. She had to."

"What? No, she did not."

"No, she did. With Angela and all the chaos from her pregnancy, it would have been too much scandal."

"Nonna?"

"Si, carina."

"You know you have to see him, right?"

Anna watched as her grandmother debated. Her grandmother placed her hands on the letters. Then with one hand put out the cigarette she was smoking. She lit another and let the smoke linger in her mouth. Her grandmother's eyes went back and forth between the letters and Anna. Liliana pursed her lips and placed one hand on forehead.

"What if I see him and those beautiful memories I have of us are ruined? I don't want to know that he has children and a beautiful wife. I can't be that for him." She took a deep breath. "I don't know."

"Nonna, you have to."

"Anna, I'm not sure. We're old now. What good can come of it?"

Anna tried to understand her grandmother's hesitation, but could not. Had she been in this situation, she wouldn't have been able to wait one second to run into her former lover's arms and kiss him everywhere. It made her miss Marco; she hadn't spoken to in nearly two weeks. She couldn't wait to tell him about the excitement in Gildone. As they sat drinking coffee, Anna noticed her grandmother's shoulders were more relaxed. Liliana held her espresso cut to her lips taking a small sip with her eyes closed. Even if Liliana could never see him, Anna was sure knowing he'd come back was enough. Finally, a promise kept.

Chapter 5

The festival was two weeks away, and all Anna could think about was how to get her grandmother to agree to a meeting. At the bakery, her grandmother was unfocused and her teaching had gone to the backburner. All of the old women in town interrupted their lessons to remind Liliana that Raffaele had returned.

"Have you seen him?" Senora Pollentino asked.

"No, I've been busy with the lessons and the bakery. Summer is just so hectic around here."

"You should see him. He wants to see you. At least, that's what I keep hearing."

"We'll see."

"Yes," the Senora said. "Well, it's a small town, you'll probably bump into him some time."

"Maybe."

"Well, Senora, here are the loaves you asked for," Anna interrupted, trying to save her grandmother from the conversation. She wasn't surprised by all the hushed excitement, given that there hadn't been this much excitement in town in years. She just felt sorry her grandmother was once again a topic of conversation. She wished it wouldn't be rude to tell them all to get over it.

The Senora left, and Liliana rolled her eyes.

"It never ends."

"I know. It's unbelievable."

"All right, well, back to your lessons."

#

Almost every day, Anna watched as her grandmother was asked questions about Raffaele, and it made her wonder what it had been like fifty years ago when he left, and then later what she endured when she was pregnant with Francesca.

"Anna, they would ask me constantly about your grandfather, and when he would come back. If it wasn't for Angela, I don't know how I would have managed."

It was true, Zia Angela had been so good about helping Liliana. Always checking up on her, even keeping the divorce situation quiet.

"If the town would have known about his wanting to divorce me, it would have been the end of this bakery."

"Why?"

"I would probably have closed it," she said, as if finalized. Lilana stared at the ground avoid eye contact with Anna.

"Nonna?"

"Si, carina."

Anna moved her head sideways to force her grandmother to look at her. She put her hand on top of Liliana's and gave it a squeeze. The bakery counter stood between them. She wanted her grandmother to clear up her thoughts, to confess.

"Just because of a divorce, you would have closed the bakery?"

Liliana shifted. Her eyes went straight to the ground.

"Well…"

"You know, your mother doesn't even know this…"

"Know what?"

Anna watched her grandmother search for the words as if looking through an old recipe book, trying to decipher the handwriting.

"When your grandfather asked me for a divorce the first time, he told me in a letter that he had remarried."

"Oh." She wasn't surprised that he had remarried; it seemed only natural that he would.

"He also told me he had four children with this woman, and that she had no clue that he was married in Italy." Liliana looked relieved to be telling this to someone.

"You mean my mother has half-brothers and sisters?"

"Yes, four of them."

"Wow."

"I wanted to tell her, but I couldn't."

"Nonna, you have to tell her."

"I know. I just don't know how."

"Nonna, if you don't tell her, you'll have done the same thing Nonna Amara did to you."

"I know. Oh God, how I know."

"She's going to be here for the festival; You could tell her then."

"I guess."

"The sooner the better. You have to tell her."

Liliana sighed. Anna was sure her grandmother was thinking of both Raffaele and Domenico. Between the questions and the confession she had to make, her grandmother had a lot to think about.

"Everything alright, Nonna?"

"Yes, I just feel overwhelmed."

"I know."

"Between your mother and Raffaele, it's too much."

"Have you decided if you're going to meet up with him

"I don't know," she mumbled. "It's just too much, too much."

Chapter 6

It was finally settled; they would meet in the center after the festival of Santa Monica had begun. Raffaele's nephew and Anna had arranged it. Roberto came to the bakery while Anna was watching it for her grandmother and the two made the arrangements.

Anna convinced Liliana that everything would be fine because of the crowds. Few would notice two old people chatting. The townspeople wouldn't think anything of it. There would be nothing to suspect.

Anna couldn't understand what her grandmother was so worried about. What did it matter that she was with Raffaele? They were old friends. There was nothing suspicious about it.

#

Francesca arrived with Davide a few days before the festival. Anna, her mother, and Angela would help with the baking needed for the festival. Anna reminded her grandmother that this would be the best time to tell Francesca about her half-brothers and sisters. It was difficult to get upset when surrounded by the scent of sugar and dough. The women walked to the bakery early the morning before the festival. Although it was early, the humidity was in full force. They arrived, glistening, and began to prep the sfogiatelle.

"So, Ma," Francesca asked, "have you decided what you're going to wear to the big meeting?"

"Oh, leave her alone. She has enough to think about," Angela reminded her.

"I didn't mean anything by it. I was just curious."

"I haven't put a moment's thought into it." Liliana looked away from Francesca.

Anna could tell she needed help, some kind of transition. She couldn't think of anything. Anna thought while the women worked in silence. Anna worked to make the dough as thin as possible without tearing it. Angela helped Liliana shape the dough into cones, and Francesca worked on the filling; her hands were too rough to work with the dough.

"It's nice being able to work without interruptions," Anna observed.

"It is," Liliana confirmed.

"Ma, you should have seen it when everyone found out Raffaele was back. Every day, they would come in and ask Nonna about it."

"Oh really?" Francesca asked. "That doesn't surprise me."

"It was crazy. Wasn't it, Nonna?"

"It reminded me of when we were young and Liliana was pregnant with you, Francesca," Angela added.

Anna watched as her grandmother gathered her strength to confess to Francesca.

"It was just like the old days," Liliana froze. Her eyes started to water.

"Ma, what is it?"

"Your father sent another letter regarding the divorce. He says he's going to sue if I don't divorce."

"Can he do that?" Francesca looked at her mother, incredulous.

"He has gotten really sick and he's been gambling to try to earn money to pay his debts." Liliana rolled her eyes.

Anna thought about the picture her mother had shown her of her grandfather, Domenico. He looked so serious and commanding. His eyes looking right into the camera. This was the same man who was betting on horses to pay his medical bills. Life had a way of being so incidental sometimes. Anna wondered how often her mother had stared at the photo imagining the type of man her father was.

"Ma, what are you going to do?"

Liliana reached out for Francesca and placed a hand on her arm. She looked down. "I just don't think I can sign the papers."

Anna watched her mother nod in understanding. She was confused.

"Why?" Anna had to know. "It makes no sense." Her voice grew louder. "Nonna, you could lose your house." She stammered. "And—and—for what?" She slammed her hands on the counter.

"She's right," Angela added. "After what he did to you?"

Liliana took a step back. She looked away and continued to cry.

"I just don't know what to do." She wiped her face. "It's all just so much."

"I know, Ma. I know." Francesca paused putting her hand on her mother's. "But, you have to do something."

The women stood in silence in the back of the bakery. The doors were locked and the only sound was of the fire heating up the oven. Angela walked over to her sister and embraced her from behind.

"It will be fine. It always is." Anna knew this wasn't true. Her grandmother moved through her life with a heavy heart. That wasn't fine. Her mother had grown up without a father. That wasn't fine. It just was. At least her grandmother had this meeting with Raffaele to look forward to. Anna hoped Liliana's meeting with Raffaele would not bring her grandmother any more pain. Her grandmother had suffered her whole life and spent it alone. She wondered if she, too, would be alone. It had been several weeks since she heard from Marco. Surely, it would be fine or maybe it would just be.

#

The preparations were complete. They closed the bakery and returned to the house for dinner. Angela and Anna cooked while Francesca set the table outside. After they finished eating, Liliana made a batch of coffee for after dinner. Her grandmother placed the cafeteria on a trivet a the center of the table. The smell of espresso lingered in the humidity.

"Ma, aren't you excited to see Raffaele? I hope you'll introduce him to us?" Francesca smiled at her mother who blushed.

"I don't know. I feel so foolish, like a schoolgirl. I'm just so embarrassed about the whole thing."

"You shouldn't be," Angela responded.

It was a relief to Anna that at least her Zia Angela understood that sometimes, it was all right to pursue your own happiness and not worry so much about what anyone else thought.

#

When the fireworks started to go off, Liliana walked towards the tree where she and Raffaele agreed to meet. He stood near the tree with his legs crossed at the ankles. His white hair rustled in the gentle summer breeze. The sound of cracking fireworks made him occasionally jolt. As he saw Liliana approach, his eyes widened. He took his hand and placed it over chest as if trying to calm the drumming of his heart. A smile spread across his face and his widened further. There he was, after fifty years, waiting for her. He pressed his lips together trying to push back his tears. Anna could see his shoulders rise and fall as he took in the humid air. He smiled again and reached his arms to Liliana.

Anna watched her grandmother hesitate to decide if she should hug or kiss him—or die. She ran her fingers through her hair and pulled on her blouse. She stood motionless. The red, green, and blue lights from the fireworks lit her face. Her grandmother looked at the ground. She took in a big gulp of air and took one step toward Raffaele. Liliana looked up at Raffaele and seeing his tears, she too bit her lip trying to quell hers. She dabbed her eyes gently trying to prevent the makeup Anna had put on her from smudging. Liliana took another step toward him. He took one toward her. The cracking of the fireworks and the cheering from the crowd overwhelmed Anna who watched as her grandmother moved closer to Raffaele. Anna too was crying. This was the type of love story for a movie. Their story was the kind that people told over long dinners and bottles of wine. It was incredible to think this type of thing actually happened, and to her grandmother of all people. Francesca watched her mother holding Davide's hand, looking back at him then at her mother.

"Is it you?" she asked.

"Is it *you?*" he replied.

They smiled and kissed one cheek, then the other.

They couldn't stop looking at each other.

"You're still beautiful." He put his hand on her cheek.

"And you've become a liar."

"Are your children here?" His eyes darted over to where Anna and Francesca were standing.

"I only had one." She looked over at Francesca, who waved. "And you? Where is your family?"

"My nephew is somewhere in the crowd."

"No, I mean your children. Your wife? Grandchildren?"

"Didn't you believe me when I said I would wait for you?"

"Of course."

Anna was overwhelmed by tears. She couldn't believe this man had actually waited for her grandmother. Liliana had needed him to save her from her loneliness and the pain. Anna wondered if only for a second if Marco loved her the way Raffaele loved her grandmother. Could she let herself suffer the way her grandmother had, knowing year after year she should let go, but couldn't? Always imagining her one true love had moved on. She wondered if Liliana felt guilty because of her marriage with Domenico. Who could blame her marrying; how could she have known about the letters? Anna felt so much pain and pity as she watched her grandmother struggle to breathe. She imagined Liliana felt pain in her chest; and though her stomach was empty, it must have been felt as if filled with heavy gray rocks and purple, pink, and yellow butterflies.

"I only wanted you," he confessed. "I don't have a wife. The one I wanted never responded."

She cried, putting her overworked hands on her wrinkled face.

"Raffaele, I—"she started but was overwhelmed with tears.

Raffaele put his hands on her back and guided her to the bench underneath the tree.

"Take your time. We have all the time now."

"This is so hard for me." She wiped her face then put her hands in her lap.

"It's hard for me too, Lili." He looked at her with a small empathic smile.

"I didn't know you had written to me." The words rushed out of her mouth.

He was confused.

"I don't understand." He wrinkled his brow and pulled away from her.

"I never got the letters," she continued. "My mother hid them from me." She went on and told him about the box of letters she kept in her nightstand. As she spoke, he moved closer to her on the bench. He moved until he was able to wrap his arm around her. She turned to him, placed her head on his chest, and sobbed.

"Lili, it's okay. We're together now."

"But we're old. It wouldn't be right."

"We can be friends? Companions?" he suggested. "You're alone, and so am I."

She could see her grandmother was too confused. She needed to think, to get away from all the fireworks and dark swinging branches of the tree they sat underneath. The air was humid and sticky, and her clothes stuck to her. She closed her eyes, trying to understand what he wanted from her.

"I don't think it would be right."

He placed his hand on her shoulder, then eased in the space next to her. They hadn't sat on that bench together in so long.

"So what if we're old? I love you."

She stood up. Anna was confused.

"I can't."

"Lili—"

"I'm sorry."

Chapter 7

Anna was shocked as she listened to her grandmother explain her reaction to Raffaele's simple request. He wanted nothing perverse, only companionship. She didn't understand her grandmother's objections.

"They could be so happy. She wouldn't be alone. What the hell?" she vented to Angela and her mother.

"You know how she is. She's always worried about what they're going to think," Angela explained.

"She's almost eighty. No one cares."

"She doesn't think like that. She thinks it's going to be a scandal. She's just like our mother."

"What you're saying is, she's going to just forget about him, leave behind a chance to be happy? Her last chance, maybe?"

Angela nodded. But that was who Liliana was.

#

The festival marked the near ending of Anna's Gildonese adventure. She had only a few weeks to convince her grandmother to change her mind. An effort her mother and aunt had told her to forget.

"Nonna, don't you think it would be smart to have him around? You two could look out for each other. Eat with each other and talk."

"Anna, they would look at me like they did when Domenico left."

"No, they wouldn't. You think they care and are judging you; they aren't. And, even *if* they are it doesn't matter. Don't you think if those people had a chance to be happy, they would take it?"

"Anna, I'm not saying I'm not going to say hi to him when I see him at mass, or in the bakery. I just don't think it's a good idea. We're old. It's inappropriate."

"Says who?"

"I'm also still married."

"Nonna, you and I both know that is ridiculous."

Liliana stood up from the kitchen table.

"I have to go prepare the sfogiatelle."

#

The summer was coming to a fast end, as summers do. The long days were getting shorter and shorter. Francesca left but promised she would return more often to make sure the house stayed clean and her grandmother was okay. Anna was only determined to help her grandmother find happiness with Raffaele; she had also almost mastered making the sfogiatelle and couldn't leave until she had made at least one perfect shell.

Raffaele stopped by the bakery every day as he had when he and Liliana were young. Each day he asked her to be his companion, and each day she reminded him that technically, she was still married to scum.

"So, when you're not married, you'll come be with me."

"Raffaele, you know I can't."

Anna noticed that even though her grandmother refused to say yes, fearing some kind of scandalous catastrophe that everyone in Gildone would talk about, she was still happy to see Raffaele every day, and this somewhat settled Anna. Still, as the fall approached, she also noticed more and more letters arrived regarding the state of Liliana's house.

"Nonna, you have to do something. You should sign the divorce papers."

"I can't. First the Raffaele business, then a divorce.... It's too much, Anna."

#

As August came to end, Anna finished planting some crops for her grandmother and showed her where she'd placed everything. There was nothing Anna could do to convince her grandmother to sign the divorce papers so she wouldn't have to lose the house or go and be with Raffaele. Her grandmother was going to do what she wanted.

Liliana watched as Anna finished packing her bags and arranged her train and bus tickets. Anna hoped her help had woken Liliana up. Her grandmother no longer appeared to be stuck in a dusty haze, but as letters from Venezuela continued to come, Anna worried Liliana would have to leave the house that had sheltered her through winters and scandal. Anna was sure it brought her grandmother some relief to know Senore Farinacci wasn't alive to see his house possibly leave Farinacci hands.

Liliana walked with Anna to the bus station.

"Carina, thank you for coming." Liliana stopped walking to hug Anna.

"I'm really glad I came. I need this."

"I needed it, too." She paused. "It's always an adventure in Gildone, eh?" She smiled at her granddaughter.

"It sure seems that way." Anna put her hand on her grandmother's arm as they kept walking. "I never thought there'd be so much excitement. I was hoping for a quiet getaway."

"It's never quiet here. There's always someone chirping about something." Liliana looked away from Anna and wiped a tear from her eye. Her shoulders drooped as she gave Anna a close-mouthed smile.

"Nonna, I'm really glad I finally learned to make some pastries."

"Well, you still have some work to do on the sfogiatelle." She sounded like her father.

"I know." Anna smiled. "It's an excuse to come back."

"Figures, just for the pastries. Forget that your grandmother isn't getting any younger." She chuckled at herself.

The engine from the bus roared. They hugged one more time and made promises to keep in touch. Liliana watched as Anna got on the bus. Too many times she had watched someone she loved getting on the bus to leave this town. She blew a kiss to Anna who was sitting by the window. As the bus left, Liliana noticed Raffaele sitting at the bar. He waved. She gave him a courteous smile and waved back, then headed to the bakery.

Chapter 8

Anna waited for the bus in Campobasso to take her back to Rome. It was nearly an hour late, but she didn't mind the wait. When she returned to Rome, she knew she would have to square things away with Marco. She had seen what holding on would eventually look like. Anna didn't want to simply abandon her life with him. There were good together, right? She thought about how he was really all she'd ever known. Maybe they just were…and just being wasn't good enough. As the bus drove past the fields of yellow and burgundy flowers, she thought about what needed to do. She was strong. She would survive. She just was not sure if she would want to.

She arrived at Termini and got onto *Linena* A and headed for the Vatican stop. She got out, surprised to see Marco standing by the stairs.

"What are you doing here?" People pushed past them as they stood on the metro platform.

"I called your mother. She told you were coming home today."

"You called my mother?" She looked at Marco. His hands were by his sides. His eyes were wide. "Why?"

"It's been really hard being away from you, Anna." She felt confined. The metro doors closed and the train started to move. "I need you."

She closed her eyes and took in the hot air. She looked back at him and started to cry.

"All summer I was waiting to hear that from you, and now that I have, I realize…" she stopped. This was the right thing to do. "Marco, we need to move on. We can't stay…stagnant." She put her hand on his chest. "I love you. I really do, but I can't do this anymore. I'm sorry."

He took her hand in his and kissed it. He nodded.

"I'm sorry, too."

The next rush of people arrived to get on the train. The doors opened and the commuters pushed past them. They stood facing each other with tears running down their faces. Anna's eyes met Marco's. Her hands shook as she reached for him again. They stood in silence, motionless and staring. The sound trains coming and going as they cried.

Chapter 9

She got off at the bus stop, Gildone was no longer green and bright as it had been in the summer. She brought her bags to the house, relieved to see her grandmother had somewhat maintained the cleaning effort. She retrieved the mail and placed it on the kitchen table. She headed to the bakery.

"Carina, help me with the sfogiatelle."

Anna was not surprised that her grandmother put her straight to work. As they prepared the pastries, Anna tried to bring up Raffaele, wondering if she could convince her grandmother to stop being so stubborn.

"No." It was that simple. "And I wish you, your mother, and Angela would stop bugging me about it."

Liliana was through with the dreams of romance and happiness. Had Fate and God decided a long time ago that she was undeserving of romance and happiness? Liliana wondered if death would be the only way for all these requests to stop. Domenico was still alive, trying to stake a claim on property he had hardly lived in; property that she had maintained while raising their daughter. Raffaele only confused her, making her question every decision she had made. She was old. She only wanted peace.

They returned to the house. Anna helped her grandmother walk up the steep slope. Liliana sat down at the table and sorted the mail. The last letter regarding the house had an Italian return address. It was from the government and had taken too long to arrive. Anna worried when she saw the official stamps and letterhead. Liliana handed it to Anna when she finished.

Mrs. Cappelino,

We regret to inform you that your husband, Domenico Cappelino, passed away June 17th 20——. He died of heart failure at the Santa Cristina Hospital in Valencia, Venezuela. The Italian government sends its condolences.

Liliana stared at the words. Tears began to dampen the official government paper. With her back to the wall, she slid down and sat on the floor. She read the letter out loud this time sending the words out into the world. Liliana could see the sun beginning to set outside, and the autumn sky was pink and lavender. She stood up wiping the tears from her face. She smiled at Anna who sat at the table watching her grandmother. Liliana looked at the kitchen and the stone walls of her house. They would forever be Farinacci walls. She picked the letter up and placed it on the table next to her cup of espresso. She felt as if bags of heavy flour had been lifted from her chest. Liliana pictured the flour rushing out of the sack landing wherever the wind blew in the air weightless and free.

Chapter 10

Anna returned to Rome, and before she could throw 500 grams of pasta, it was Christmas. Anna was relearning how to cook for one. She had prepped the broccoli and sautéed them with garlic and oil, and she had drizzled them with some lemon juice. She stood with her elbows on the counter and waited for the water to boil to throw the farfalle pasta in. The phone rang.

"*Pronto.*"

"Anna, it's me." Her mother spoke quickly. "Did you hear?"

She didn't get the chance to answer.

"Raffaele had a stroke."

"Is he going to be okay? How is Nonna?"

"She refuses to go see him."

Anna rolled her eyes.

"Maybe if you talk to her."

#

Anna called and called, letting the phone ring in her ear. Her grandmother was avoiding them, not wanting to hear common sense. She tried calling Angela, whose only response was: "She's eighty years old, she does what she wants." She kept calling, and when she finally got a hold of Liliana, the conversation was brief.

"*Pronto.*"

"Nonna?"

"Sì?"

"I just heard. Nonna, are you okay?"

"I'm fine." She took a breath. "I just feel bad about the whole thing."

"I know." She heard her grandmother sigh. "Well, are you going to go and see him?"

It was clear to Anna that Liliana was annoyed her family wouldn't leave her alone. She wasn't ready to go and see him, and they refused to let her alone.

"I'm not ready, and I don't know why."

She was tired of being held prisoner by it all.

Chapter 11

Raffaele's nephew hadn't called to tell her about the stroke. She'd heard about it as she returned from the bakery moments after it happened. She could hear the ambulance and watched as the paramedic closed the back door and hurried inside. It drove off; the rectangular vehicle moved past the twists in the mountain road with ease.

"What happened?" she asked.

"Raffaele," Senore Carriero replied.

"What about him?"

"He fell down. He was having a little wine, and *pahf,* he hit the floor."

"Is he going to be all right?"

"Who knows?" He held his fists up shaking them the sky.

She rolled her eyes at him, then walked back to her house. She entered and sat in silence. When the phone rang a couple of hours later, it was Raffaele's nephew.

"He's asking for you."

"I don't know." It was all she could say.

She listened to Anna plead with her about going.

"Nonna, this is your chance to make peace with the whole thing."

Liliana nodded even though Anna couldn't see her do so.

"Anna, I'm getting on the bus this afternoon. Don't worry, I know what I have to do."

Epilogue

She arrived at the hospital, stood at the nurse's station, and asked for Raffaele's room. An older nurse escorted her to his room. Machines were hooked up to him and tubes and wires seemed to be feeding off of him.

"He can't speak, and the doctor isn't sure if he recognizes anyone. You are the only visitor he's had besides that sweet nephew of his."

She thanked the nurse.

Liliana looked at him, and with her rough, overworked hands, she traced the lines of his face and wept.

"I'm sorry, *amore*."

She said it only once, hoping he had heard it somehow.

She sat with him, listening to the tubes do his breathing. Hours passed. She looked at him, hardly recognizing the man who had waited and waited for her. He was a good man. He was such a good man. A man who had loved only her.

She kissed his forehead, then his lips.

She stood up as if moving through a ball of dough. She turned back only once, then walked away from him, never knowing she could.

Acknowledgements

This novel was ten years in the making. I never expected it to see the light of day, and it probably wouldn't have if it weren't for my one and only, Justin. Marrying you has been, by far, the best decision of my life. From this novel's inception, through its, let's call it the "hibernation" period, querying, and revision, you have believed that this book needed to be out there on bookshelves and in the hands of readers. Thank you for sharing in my vision of being a writer and for helping me get up after the many falls. Thank you for standing behind me, cheering me on, and supporting me (in all the ways). I don't know what I did in a past life to deserve you in this one, but for you, I am the most thankful. I have said this before, and I will say it again: *you are my favorite human.*

To my little boo, this book is so much about motherhood's glory and hardships. It's about women and their sacrifices and some of what it takes to raise little humans into kind, independent big humans. I wrote it long before you made me a momma, but having you has taught me so much about motherhood. You have brought so much joy, light, and silliness into our lives, (and let's face it, we're all obsessed with *Star Wars* now because of you). You came into my life at one of my darkest times, and your light has been so beautifully bright. Thank you, sweet boy.

Mother, I miss you every day. You were a great mother, and when readers think of a character as stoic and strong, I want them to know those moments of silent, persistent strength were inspired by you. You taught me how to love being a woman in a world where being female is hard and frustrating and oftentimes, gut-wrenching. Thank you, because, honestly, being a woman kicks ass, and I know that because of you.

Courtney Watson thank you for being my best friend and cheerleader. Without your unrelenting positivity and encouragement, this writer's life would be dreadful. Many a night you dropped what you were working on to help me with this book. I'm also so grateful for you and our shared love of bubbly. Cheers!

Ayse Papatya Bucak, when I started this novel as an M.F.A. candidate at Florida Atlantic University, you told me I was writing a 300-page novel. I remember shaking my head telling you that was not true. I don't know why I doubted you, but you were right. Thank you for seeing what this novel could be and for giving me the tools to make it what it is. I feel so privileged to have been your student.

Zia Fiore, this novel would be impossible without you. Your story inspired so much of this novel. You are one of the fiercest women I have ever met, and your zeal has always left a big impression on me. I'm glad we met during my formative years because I'm pretty sure I got some of my firecracker power from you. I'm so grateful to have known you and to be your niece.

To my father, Phil Panzera, and sisters Michelle and Joanna Panzera, thank you for supporting my dream and letting me call you to read pages of my writing out loud so I can make it better. Daddy, thank you for answering my questions about Italy and telling me about our amazing family.

Maggie, Lucy, and Frank Panzera, thank you for all your help. Your ability to remember nitty gritty details and share them with me whenever I asked was instrumental in shaping this novel.

Debbie and Steven Fiedler, my wonderful in-laws, first thank you for your incredible son, he is a great man because of you, but also thank you for helping me with Little Man when I needed time to write and revise. Knowing my son was safe and happy with you makes writing and mom-ing possible. I am so blessed to be part of your family.

Kristen Fox, thank you for your support and feedback. Your insight and help made revising this novel a *little* less daunting. I love you and am so grateful to call you my friend.

Thank you to the English department at Florida Atlantic University and the University of Miami for training me and preparing me to be a writer. I have been so blessed to receive such a great education from phenomenal educators.

And finally, to the team at Unsolicited Press, I am eternally grateful that you believed in this book. When I got the email from Summer accepting my manuscript for publication, I was unsure if my decision to write was a good one. The night before getting the acceptance, I had thrown a raging pity party. It was one of my better shindigs. The UP team gave me incredible feedback and pushed me to be a better writer. Also, Summer, thank you for endless patience and for giving me the time to make this book be the best it could be. Thank you.

About the Author

Gloria Panzera is a writer and teacher. She earned her Master of Fine Arts in Fiction writing from Florida Atlantic University. Her work has appeared in *2 Bridges Review*, *The Inquisitive Eater*, *One Forty Fiction*, *Gravel*, and *Crack the Spine*, among others. *With All My Love, I Wait* is her first novel. She currently teaches creative writing and English in Charlotte, North Carolina where she lives with her husband and son.

About the Press

Unsolicited Press is based in Portland, Oregon and publishes poetry, fiction, and creative nonfiction from award-winning authors.

Learn more at www.unsolicitedpress.com.

www.ingramcontent.com/pod-product-compliance
Lightning Source LLC
Chambersburg PA
CBHW050345190726
48284CB00007BB/2154